Readers love
RICK R. REED

Bigger Love

"A tone of authentic tenderness and yearning, completely without artifice, suffuses Reed's engaging Appalachian tale of high-school gay love."

— Booklist

Big Love

"*Big Love* is a heart warming, heart breaking story about what it means to be gay in modern America."

—Divine Magazine

"I was blown away by how good this book was and how it truly wound its way around my heart.... This is one of those books you remember years to come."

—Inked Rainbow Reviews

Sky Full of Mysteries

"The writing here is stellar, with a plot that takes us on a path we _____ highly recommend _____ tars."

_____ views

By RICK R. REED

Bashed
Big Love • Bigger Love
Blink
Blue Umbrella Sky
Caregiver
Chaser • Raining Men
The Couple Next Door
A Dangerous Game
Dinner at Fiorello's
Dinner at Jack's
Dinner at Home
Dinner at the Blue Moon Café
With Vivien Dean: Family Obligations
Homecoming
Hungry for Love
Husband Hunters
I Heart Boston Terriers
Legally Wed
Lost and Found
M4M
An Open Window
The Perils of Intimacy
Simmer
Sky Full of Mysteries
Tricks

DREAMSPUN DESIRES
With Vivien Dean: #15 – Stranded with Desire

Published by DREAMSPINNER PRESS
www.dreamspinnerpress.com

BLUE UMBRELLA SKY

RICK R. REED

Published by
DREAMSPINNER PRESS

5032 Capital Circle SW, Suite 2, PMB# 279,
Tallahassee, FL 32305-7886 USA
www.dreamspinnerpress.com

Blue Umbrella Sky
© 2019 Rick R. Reed.

Cover Art
© 2019 Reese Dante.
http://www.reesedante.com
Cover content is for illustrative purposes only and any person depicted on the cover is a model.

Mass Market Paperback ISBN: 978-1-64108-069-9
Trade Paperback ISBN: 978-1-64080-877-5
Digital ISBN: 978-1-64080-876-8
Library of Congress Control Number: 2018944473
Mass Market Paperback published March 2019
v. 1.0

Printed in the United States of America
∞
This paper meets the requirements of
ANSI/NISO Z39.48-1992 (Permanence of Paper).

For Nicholas, my shining light in all the darkness, my finest and best legacy, the creation of which I'm most proud.
I love you, son.

"There is something beautiful about a blank canvas, the nothingness of the beginning that is so simple and breathtakingly pure. It's the paint that changes its meaning and the hand that creates the story. Every piece begins the same, but in the end they are all uniquely different."

—*Piper Payne*

"I once had a thousand desires, but in my one desire to know you, all else melted away."

—*Rumi*

"If you keep picking at that scab on your heart, it won't heal."

—*Antonia Perdu*

"I have always loved the desert. One sits down on a desert sand dune, sees nothing, hears nothing. Yet through the silence something throbs and gleams…."

—*Antoine de Saint-Exupéry,
The Little Prince*

CHAPTER 1

MILT GRABAUR stared out the window of his trailer, wondering how much worse it could get.

The deluge poured down, gray, almost obscuring his neighbors' homes and the barren desert landscape beyond. The rain hammered on his metal roof, sounding like automatic gunfire. Milt shivered a little, thinking of that old song, "It Never Rains in Southern California."

He leaned closer to the picture window, pressing his hand against the glass and whispering to himself, "But it pours."

That window had given him his daily view for the last six months, ever since he'd packed up a life's worth of belongings and made his way south and west to Palm Springs and the Summer Winds Mobile Home Community. This same picture window, almost every single day, had shown him only endless blue skies and sunshine. An errant cloud or a jet contrail would occasionally break up the field of electric blue, but other than

that, it was azure perfection. Milt reveled in it. He'd
begun to think these expanses of blue, lit up by golden
illumination, would never cease.

Until today.

At about three o'clock, that blue sky, for the first
time, was overcome with gray, a foreboding mass of
bruised clouds. Milt wondered, because of his experience in the desert so far, if the clouds would be only
that—foreboding. The magical gods of the Coachella
Valley would, of course, sweep away those frowning
and depressing masses of imminent precipitation with
a wave of their enchanted hands.

Surely.

But the sky continued to darken, seemingly unaware of Milt's fanciful imagining and yearnings. At
last the once-blue dome above him became almost like
night in midafternoon and the first heavy drops—fat
beads of water—began to fall, first a slow sprinkle,
where Milt could count the seconds between drops,
then faster and faster, until the raindrops combined into
one single and, Milt had to admit, *terrifying* roar.

And then an unfamiliar sound—the drumroll and
cymbal crash of thunder. The sky, moments after, lit up
with brilliant white light.

The rain fell in earnest. Torrents of the stuff.

The other trailers, his neighbors, nearly vanished
in the relentless gray downpour. The wind howled,
sending the rain capriciously sideways every few seconds. The palm trees in his front yard swayed and bent
with the ruthless gusts, testimony to their strength, despite their appearance of being stalklike and weak. The
wind tore dry husks of bark from them.

At first Milt was unconcerned, thinking the
rain could only do good. It would bless the parched

succulents, cacti, and palms that dotted the rocky, sandy landscape of the park, maybe even bring them to colorful life, forcing a brilliant desert flower, here and there, to bloom. His decade-old Honda Civic, parked next to the trailer, would get a wash, the thick layer of sand and dust chased away, almost pressure-cleaned.

For the half a year he'd been here, Milt had been amazed at how clean everything could look when, in actuality, anything outdoors was quickly covered in a veneer of fine sand, almost like gritty dust. Milt was forever wiping off his patio furniture, cleaning the glass surfaces of his car. But this minor inconvenience was more than outweighed by the stunning and almost surreal appearance of the Coachella Valley and the desert, a wild beauty which far surpassed anything even an optimistic Milt had dreamed of when he had made up his mind, somewhat suddenly, to shed his old life in Ohio and move out to Southern California.

He stared out at the gusts of wind, the flashes of lightning, and the almost-blinding downpour and realized he had no idea it could be like this. The trailer park was smack up against the San Jacinto mountain range, and Milt realized with horror that not only would the little park suffer from the copious water falling from the sky, but it would also be the beneficiary, like it or not, of runoff as it came hurtling down the mountain face.

As if to confirm his notion, Milt gasped as he noticed the street in front of his trailer.

It was no longer a street.

Not really.

No, now it was a creek. A creek notable for its rushing rapids. Water was speeding by at an unprecedented pace. Milt sucked in some air as he saw a lawn chair go by, buoyed up by the current. Then a plastic end table. An inflatable pool toy—a swan—that Milt supposed was in the right place at the right time. But the damp throw pillows whizzing by, like soggy oyster crackers in soup, were not.

Milt turned to look behind him at the sound of a whimper.

"Oh, what's the matter, sweetheart?" He held out a beseeching hand to the gray-and-white pit bull mix he'd picked up from the Palm Springs Animal Shelter over on Mesquite the first week he'd gotten here. "It's okay."

She looked ferocious but was a big softie, easily frightened, shy, and with a disposition that made Mother Teresa look like a terrorist. Ruby, he'd called her on a whim, in honor of the kind lady that lived two doors down from him when he was a little boy back in Summitville, Ohio. *That* Ruby, like this one, had always been kind but retiring, shying from the slightest spotlight.

This Ruby, right now, was terrified, her tail between her legs, backing toward the shadowy corners of the room, eyes wide with fear. Milt reached out, trying to grab the frightened dog, but she scurried away and dashed out of sight down the narrow hallway leading to his bedroom, nails clattering, slipping and sliding on the tile floor. Milt sighed, knowing exactly what she was doing even though he couldn't see her—scurrying under his bed to cower among the dust bunnies and cast-off shoes.

It would take hours—and treats—to coax her out. Milt knew from experience….

He returned his attention to the storm raging outside, which showed no signs of abating.

Plus—and this made Milt groan—there was a new wrinkle to the carnage. Not only were the streets around his trailer now rapidly flowing rivers; Milt also realized with horror he was about to get flooded.

He gazed down on standing water several inches deep spread out across his patio. It covered the outdoor rugs he'd bought, with their whimsical cactus design, soaking them like washcloths. It rose up the sides of his patio furniture. Milt swore he could see it getting higher and higher.

Worst of all, Milt watched the water hover just outside the sliding glass doors, waiting, perhaps, for an invitation to come inside.

Ah, the hell with it, the water seemed to say, *why wait for an invitation? This party needs crashing!*

And it began to seep in.... A little at first, and then faster and faster, until his entire floor was covered.

Milt involuntarily cried out, voice high-pitched and terrified, nothing like the butch forty-two-year-old he thought himself. "Help! Flood! Somebody, please!" The cry was pure panic. Logically, he knew no one would hear.

What that helper would do, Milt had no idea, but he simply wanted someone to be with him in his predicament. The thought flitted across his consciousness that he'd been here six months, and it wasn't until today and the advent of a rainstorm of biblical proportions that he realized he didn't want to be alone. He swore as warm water covered his bare feet at the exact moment his power went out, plunging his little sanctuary into murky dark.

And at this very unnerving moment, Milt realized—gratefully—someone just might have heard his pleas for help. There was a pounding at the back door, rattling the glass jalousie panes. He turned, confused for a moment—he'd cast himself as a sole survivor, a man against nature, alone.

The pounding continued. A voice. "Hey! You okay in there?"

Milt crossed the living room and the small galley kitchen to get to the back door. But when he opened it, there was no one there. The wind pushed at him, mocking, and the rain sent a drenching spray against him. Despite getting soaked, Milt leaned out, gripping the door's frame with both hands for balance, and looked around.

Even though the covering of storm clouds had made it seem as though a dusky twilight had fallen, he could see that there was no one there.

He wondered if he'd imagined the knocking and the voice. He really didn't know his neighbors, having kept to himself since he'd moved out here because he just wasn't ready to connect with others again. He'd given so much to his Corky during those final tortured months…. Sometimes Milt felt he had nothing left to give anyone again *ever*.

And a dog, cowering and bashful as she might be, had been company enough.

His little reverie was shattered by a second round of knocking, this time at the sliding glass doors in his living room. "Okay, so I'm not hearing things." Milt turned away from the back door and headed to the sliders.

Outside, a young man stood, drenched from head to toe, in a pair of neon-pink board shorts and, well, nothing else. *Maybe there's flip-flops.* Milt couldn't see the guy's feet. His jaw dropped as he hurried to open the door. In spite of all that was going on—the storm, the flood, the risk of his home being destroyed—he couldn't help his thoughts, notions he'd decided long ago died within him.

I am looking at an angel; that's all there is to it. He's going to sweep me away in those muscular arms, lifting me right up to heaven and setting me down gently next to my Corky.

Milt shook his head. A short burst of laughter escaped him, almost as if someone else were chuckling in his living room with him.

The guy *was* handsome, a tanned and buff dreamboat. Corky would have loved him, saying, once upon a time, that looks like this boy's should be illegal, or at least sinful. Milt smiled.

Even though his hair was plastered to his head, Milt could tell it was thick and luxurious—right now the color of dark wheat, but Milt was certain that in dryer moments, it was as gold as the pure, unfiltered sunshine Milt had grown accustomed to being greeted by every morning. He had a body that made Milt, if only for a moment, forget the storm *and* the fact that he was a widower, still grieving nearly a year after losing his man. Muscles, smooth bronze skin, and a six-pack had the power of oblivion, of taking precedence over everything else.

Stop, he mentally chastised himself. He flung open the slider, noticing the rain had—at last—slowed to a patter and the winds had died down almost completely. Milt, though, couldn't seem to put lips and tongue together to form a greeting or ask a question or to even say anything at all. His eyebrows came together like two caterpillars possessed of their own will.

"Hey there, man. I heard you calling out for help." He jerked a thumb over his shoulder. "I live in the unit behind you." He smiled, revealing electric-white teeth that made Milt's thoughts go even more blank or even more lascivious, he wasn't sure which. He shivered.

The guy gave Milt a more tentative smile, the type you'd give to the kindly neighbor down the street who'd just emerged from home wearing nothing but a pair of saddle shoes and a big smile. Milt wondered if the guy thought he was encountering a person who couldn't speak, or maybe someone whose mind had completely deserted him. Lord knew Milt was familiar enough with people like that, having only very recently seen to every need of a person just like that.

"Are you okay, buddy?"

Milt managed a smile, despite the fact that his feet squished on the soaked carpeting. *Oh Lord, is everything ruined? How much is this going to cost? Is it going to wipe me out?* "Yeah," Milt sputtered. He glanced behind him. "It looks as though I'm getting flooded." There appeared to be at least a couple of inches of water covering the floor of his trailer. He groaned.

The young man leaned in to survey the damage and gave a low whistle. "Yikes!" He leaned back out so he could face Milt. "Bet you didn't think you needed to worry about flooding in the desert?"

Milt shook his head. "Well, it wasn't foremost." He glanced behind him again, feeling like his sanctuary had been violated—as it indeed had. And what fresh hell would spring forth from the damage? "What am I gonna do?"

"Well, my opinion is you need to get yourself the hell out of there. As I said, I'm right behind you, *up* the mountain a tad, so I'm still dry. You wanna grab some of your stuff just in case and come on over?"

"Stuff?"

"Yeah, man, like, I don't know, a laptop, maybe? Family pictures? Important papers? You know, just in case. The stuff you'd run out of here with if the place caught on fire."

"Oh, right." Milt sighed. "This is awfully kind of you."

"Hey, we're neighbors. At Summer Winds, we look out for each other. I've been wanting to meet you, anyway. Sucks that it has to be under these circumstances. But come on, I've got a dry house, air-conditioning, and enough candy to send you into a diabetic coma." He laughed.

Milt stood, his mind beating a hasty retreat. He shouldn't feel indecisive, but he did.

"Or if you have other plans...," the man finally said. "Indoor pool party?"

"No. No! I'd love to come over." Milt looked around his place once more. Most of his stuff was up high enough that it wouldn't get wet, unless the trailer toppled over or something, but there was one thing he couldn't just leave behind. "I need to get Ruby."

"Ruby?"

"My girl, my dog!" Milt snapped, as if his visitor should know. He immediately regretted his tone, but his neighbor simply seemed to be taking his dire straits way too lightly.

"Ruby. Cute name. I've seen you walking her. She's sweet. Go grab her. She's welcome too. Animals of all varieties are welcome in my crib." He winked. "I used to have a dog myself, a Yorkie, Bergamot, that thought he was a Doberman." He frowned. "But he passed away last winter. Coyote got him."

Milt jerked a little in horror. "I'm sorry."

Milt couldn't imagine losing his dog—he'd already fallen hopelessly in love with Ruby. He felt a deep-seated twinge of empathy. "The storm shook her up. Let me just see if I can coax her out from under the bed." Milt didn't think the task would be too tough, since it was now wet under the bed and Ruby hated water. He turned and started away, sloshing through the hateful water. Midstream, so to speak, he changed his mind and turned back.

He held out a hand. "I'm sorry. Milt. Milt Grabaur. I'd invite you in, but my place, as you can see, isn't exactly presentable." He laughed and then felt like bursting into tears.

"If you knew I was coming, you'd have baked a cake? A sponge cake?" He snorted and shook Milt's hand with a big calloused paw. "Billy Blue."

Milt smiled. "Seriously?"

Billy shrugged. "Yeah, my mom and dad had a great sense of humor. Or thought I was destined for the stage, instead of cashier at Trader Joe's. The advantage of a name like mine, silly as it is, is that people tend not to forget it."

"I think it's a lovely name." Milt met Billy Blue's gaze—and thought how fortuitous it was that his irises matched the color of his last name. *And you're a lovely man. Handsome, built like a brick shithouse—and sweet as pie.*

"I'll be right back with Ruby." He turned and this time did manage to slosh to the very rear of the trailer, where his wood-paneled master bedroom awaited. Before he even stooped down in the grimy water to coax, he began talking to Ruby. "Good girl. Nothin' to be ascared of, honey," Milt said in his most soothing voice, cadence and words dredged up from his boyhood

memories of living near the river in the foothills of the
Appalachians, in the northern panhandle of West Vir-
ginia. He squatted down, wincing a little as his knees
came into contact with the spongy shag carpeting he'd
hoped to replace one day, and lifted the bottom of the
comforter, which was stained dark from the water.

Underneath the bed there was only a couple of
inches of water, a pair of Keen sandals, and a metal
storage box that contained Milt's "toys"—and we're
not talking Fisher-Price here.

There was no Ruby. Nor any other living creature.

Milt got to his feet, groaning, and took stock of the
entire bedroom, thinking perhaps Ruby had retreated
to a corner or hidden behind the chest of drawers. But
she was nowhere to be found, not even in the adjacent
bathroom, which looked now as though Milt had taken
a long, long shower and had simply not bothered to turn
the water off.

Knowing she wouldn't be there, but checking anyway, Milt opened the frosted glass shower door to find
it empty.

He made a tour of the trailer, getting more and
more anxious with each step, with each empty nook
and cranny. "Ruby?" he called out several times, each
time his voice growing louder, as though sheer volume
would make her appear.

But she didn't.

And the thoughtlessly left-open back door gave
testimony to what had most likely happened. The poor
terrified girl had probably tried to escape that way, running headlong into a fate worse than she was trying to
escape. Milt hurried to the open door, peering out onto
his little patio, hoping against hope she'd be out there,

stub of a tail sending up splashes as she looked mournfully at him.

But Ruby was gone.

Milt felt as though his heart would break.

He closed the door behind him, sighing and wondering if he should leave it open, just in case she tried to return. Return to what? A trailer flooded with filthy—and probably bacteria-ridden—water?

He moved back to the sliders, looking over Billy's broad shoulders, hoping Ruby would appear on the doused desert landscape.

Billy smiled at Milt's return. "Dog?" he wondered.

Milt's breath caught. The day, or not really the day but only, really, the past few minutes, had been a disaster. *Disasters happen fast and savage in Palm Springs.* He wasn't sure he could speak without bursting into tears, without chastising himself for his own carelessness.

If only I hadn't left that damn door open.

"She's nowhere to be found." Milt shrugged.

Billy frowned, and his gaze seemed to reach out to Milt in sympathy, which made Milt want to cry even more. "She'll turn up." Billy changed his expression to a reassuring smile. "She's got it good—a man all to herself, and I assume a limitless supply of treats." He winked. "I wish I could say the same."

Ah, so he's one of us. I thought so, but one doesn't want to assume. "I'm sure you're right," Milt said, although he wasn't sure at all.

"You still want to come over? I got carnitas cooking in the Crock-Pot. Homemade tortillas. I may be blond, but I cook like the locals."

Milt managed a smile. The thought of food made his stomach turn, thinking of Ruby running around out there somewhere—with threats like coyotes, black widow spiders, and rattlesnakes all around, just to name a few. She might look fierce, but Milt feared she wouldn't last long up against the desert's more formidable predators.

At least it's not raining anymore.

"You wanna gather some stuff up?"

Milt shook his head. "It'll be okay." Barefoot, morose, he stepped through the sliders and outside.

"Atta boy. We'll get settled over at my place, and then we can do a little search-and-rescue mission. I'm sure she's not far away."

"I hope not." Milt followed Billy Blue into the unseasonably damp day. Steam was already beginning to rise off surfaces not under water.

The sun was beginning to come out again, revealing blue skies.

Milt couldn't see it, though.

CHAPTER 2

"I DON'T know what I'm going to do," Milt said in response to his best friend, Dane Bernard's, question. Tugging at his black necktie, he longed for some air, some clarity. An escape. Yes, he just wanted to be away…

… from this nightmare

… from this death

… from this reality, a reality that revealed a dark future, one that seemed, right now, to be devoid of hope.

Where was the life Milt had planned? You know, the one that included growing old with Corky, that clichéd notion of being in rocking chairs, side by side, fingers intertwined.

"You don't have to decide right now. You have plenty of time. And nothing, really, has to change. You have a wonderful community here—a great network of friends who love you dearly. Students who look up to you." Dane, a big man, Milt's best friend and coteacher at Summitville High School, had experienced his own loss of a spouse a few years ago when his wife, Katie, had perished in a car accident out on Route 11. Dane squeezed Seth's hand and then let go. "And of course, you can always count on Seth and me to be there whenever you need us." He grinned a little. "And even when you don't, to the point where we become irritants." He shrugged. "Give yourself time. You'll know what to do when the time is right."

"Said by a person for whom everything changed when their life partner passed." Milt raised an eyebrow. He sat across a folding card table from Dane at the American Legion hall, which Milt had rented for the after-funeral lunch. There'd been a buffet of rigatoni in meat sauce, fried chicken, and tossed salad. A Texas sheet cake waited on a table for someone to be the first to cut into it. There was punch and, for the drinkers, beer and horrible red wine in boxes.

Dane nodded. After his wife died, Dane had come out, to the school's and the town's shock. He was now married to yet another teacher at the high school, Seth Wolcott. The three men were, far as Milt knew, the only gays at the school, at least on the teaching end. He had suspicions about Betty Beaver, who ran the school cafeteria.

Milt, Dane, and Seth were best friends—not because they had the unusual distinction of being the only gays in the village, so to speak, but because each was possessed of a singularly large organ.

Their hearts.

"I have no regrets about being married to Katie. You know that."

"You got the kids." Milt nodded, as if that rationalization was obvious. Dane had a teenage son and daughter. Both were smart, well-adjusted, and turning out to be gorgeous—both inside and out.

"Yeah, that's true. I got the kids, but that's not the only reason." Dane chuckled. "That's the reason most people think, now that they know—and I know—I'm gay, but I really loved her, Milt. In my own way, as much as I love Seth. I miss her every day." Dane studied Milt, and Milt could see Dane's eyes growing shinier, which caused sympathetic tears to well up within Milt's own eyes. He was feeling extremely vulnerable these days.

"I'm gonna miss Corky every day. I can't imagine a world without him in it." Milt shrugged. "Hell, I already miss him." He sniffed. "Actually, I'd been pining away for him since long before he passed. He was gone…." Milt's voice trailed off, and he shook his head, breath fluttering. He gripped the table, all the air in the room suddenly sucked out of it.

Finally Milt got control of his tears and continued. "He was actually gone that summer day, a couple of years ago, when he told me he couldn't find his sunglasses." Milt wanted to weep at the memory and wished he were alone instead of in an American Legion hall full of sympathetic and sad faces. Instead of crying, though, Milt dug down deep and summoned a chuckle. "How we laughed about it that day, because they were right on top of his big old bald head!" Milt laughed some more but then quickly grew serious. "But this was the *second* time we'd laughed about it. We cracked up about it *again* because it had only been about ten minutes before that we'd laughed over it when he'd confronted me with the very same problem." He looked pointedly at Dane. "I always remember that moment, silly as it might sound. But that's when I started to get scared that something was wrong. His mom and his aunt, her sister, had both passed from Alzheimer's. He was always worried about it coming to him. Who knew it would rush right up to him, and him so young?" Milt looked away at the people in the hall, with its knotty pine paneling, American flags, its black-and-white checked tile floor where, once upon a time, he and Corky had had the courage to slow dance in front of his coworkers at a Christmas party. *That* was a moment he'd never forget either—proudly holding his big, strong bearded man in his arms as they waltzed around the floor to Al Green's "Let's Stay Together." Milt recalled the line about wanting to spend a life with that special person. He didn't know, that Christmas just four or five years ago, how short their life together was destined to be.

Milt stared down at his paper plate. He picked up a chicken leg and took a bite. The meat tasted like paper or Styrofoam—like nothing. He chewed slowly, though, telling himself he had to hold it together for just an hour or two more. Then he could go home—to their little redbrick ranch overlooking the Ohio River— and break down. He could stare at the muddy water as it curved, serpentine, through their town and watch the snowflakes melt as they landed on its surface. He could imagine warmer, happier times when he and Corky would wend their way down the banks on what they thought of as their secret trail to skinny-dip on hot summer afternoons from the pebbled shore.

He'd savor these memories alone.

When he looked up again, he forced himself to smile. And Dane, the relief apparent on his face, smiled back. He squeezed Milt's hand. "As I said, you don't need to make any decisions now. Everything can wait.

Don't rush yourself. This is a vulnerable time. You're in no condition to make big choices." Dane reached over to pat Milt's hand. "Nothing has to change."

But everything has changed, Milt thought. *Everything.*

Dane's words felt like a weight pressing against Milt's chest, sucking away his air. No. Everything *couldn't* wait.

Things had been waiting, waiting, waiting for the past two years as Corky deteriorated. The forgetfulness was a joke at first, then more and more terrifying as the disease cruelly progressed. And then came the personality changes and watching his big kind bear of a husband become mean. That was something Milt hadn't been prepared for. His big lovable bear was the type to trap a spider and release it outdoors rather than kill it. And yet, at his worst, Corky had punched and slapped Milt more times than Milt had ever let anyone know, hiding his bruises when he could and, when he couldn't, concocting stories to explain them innocently away. But he knew Corky hadn't been himself. And then, faster and faster, everything went to shit, with Corky no longer knowing who Milt was—and that hurt far worse than any fist to the jaw—and then his constant, and sometimes successful, attempts to escape their home. Dressed or not.

Putting him in a home broke Milt's heart. But he just couldn't handle things alone anymore. The move to the home, he told himself, was for Corky's own safety. And it was. It really was. But it was also for Milt's sanity. Still, it just about killed him to see Corky there, in that antiseptic place with the wheelchair-bound, the bright, artificial Muzak, the smell of Lysol barely masking the odors of shit and piss.

Fortunately—or not—that almost-final letting go and putting him in care was for only a very short time. Once there, Corky quickly declined—and moved on for good.

In only two weeks.

"No, man, *nothing* can wait. My life has been on hold for so long, I feel like I can't fuckin' breathe. I need a change." Milt gazed desperately about the room, feeling trapped here. This luncheon wasn't a comfort, despite the home-cooked food, the kind faces, and the consoling words. It was a reminder that he still existed in a cage.

Dane cocked his head. "You're not gonna leave us, are you?" There was real despair on Dane's face, and Milt almost swept in with false reassurance, words he knew Dane expected to hear. Milt had always been the kind of guy who thought of others first—not that there was anything wrong with that, except when you did it at the expense of yourself.

Milt finally realized, in his early forties but not too late, that he needed to secure his own oxygen mask first before he would be any good to anyone else.

"You don't want me to go?"

"Of course I don't! You're my best friend, Milt. Who would Seth and I go to lunch and a movie at the Boardman Mall with? Who would help us run the popcorn stand at football games in the fall?" Dane laughed. "And who will cook us that damn chili you're always saying is the best in the world?" Dane, still smiling, wiped a tear out of the corner of his eye. "Don't tell Seth I said it, but it really is. The best in the world." Dane stared at him, hard. "Really, man, we'd be lost without you."

Milt didn't know what to say to that. Well, he knew what to say, but he felt like he'd be heartless and cruel if he said it.

After a few moments, though, Dane saved him. "I'm so sorry, buddy. I'm being a selfish dick. I shouldn't make you feel bad. What a shit I am! What—what are you thinking of doing? Um, now that things are different?"

Milt looked for a minute out the big plate glass window at the front of the Legion hall, where snowflakes were beginning to fall. Pretty, big, and fluffy, but they'd make everyone's drive home on the windy, hilly roads of Summitville treacherous. They told a tale of biting wind, cold that froze the tip of your nose, cold that hurt.

"Palm Springs has three hundred and fifty days of sunshine a year," Milt blurted out.

Dane followed Milt's gaze to the window—the snow falling fast, the edges of the glass etched with frost. "Sounds wonderful." He ate a few bites of pasta, then said, "Wait. You're thinking of moving out there? To Southern California?"

Truth be told, Milt hadn't seriously considered it until right this very moment. In the last months of Corky's decline, when autumn was morphing into winter, with its sleety gray skies and bare, leafless trees, he'd imagined, in a vague way, a place that was sunny and always warm. Maybe oceanfront on the Gulf coast of Florida. Naples was nice. Or maybe he could become an expat and get himself down to Mexico and the Yucatán peninsula. He and Corky had had one of their best vacations ever there, renting a beach house in the little village of Puerto Morelos. All they did was lie by the pool, drink margaritas, make love, walk hand in hand on the beach, and read a book a day. Heaven.

In the lobby of the nursing home, just before Corky passed, Milt had picked up an old issue of *Travel and Leisure* magazine, drawn by its cover—a field of Joshua trees with a range of rusty mountains, rocky and austere, rising up majestically behind them to meet the electric blue sky. Milt thought the trees looked like something out of Dr. Seuss. The magazine had contained a story about Palm Springs and the desert—the beauty of the area and the abundant sunshine, its spiritual presence. There were dazzling photos of sun-drenched mountain ranges, cacti, vibrant desert blooms, and blue skies, nothing but blue skies....

He'd set the magazine down when an aide came to tell him Corky was awake and would he like to see him?

He hadn't thought anything more of Palm Springs until this very moment. But the thought had stayed with him, tucked away in his subconscious until today, when he realized, in his grief, that despite being devastated by a crushing loss, he was also free.

And now, seeing that article seemed very much like fate.

"Yeah," he said, his voice becoming more confident and convinced as he went on. "Yeah, I am. If I can make the finances work, I just might move out to Palm Springs." Another notion seized him. "Maybe take an extended sabbatical and write that novel I've always considered doing."

A vision rose up in Milt's mind's eye—a dusty, rock-strewn trail, the earth beneath his feet sun-washed, ochre, heading upward, the side of a blue-gray mountain. A relentless sun beat down, making each step both effort and joy, making his heart pound in his chest, reminding him he was alive.

His vision stopped when Dane's husband, Seth, with his curly-haired handsomeness and winsome smile, interrupted. He sat down at the table with a paper plate loaded with chicken breasts and pasta, and Milt hated him for just a moment—to be able to eat like that and maintain what was obviously a thirty-inch waist.

He smiled at Milt and gave Dane a little wink. "What are you two talking about?"

Dane spoke before Milt had the chance. "Milt here is moving to Palm Springs."

Seth laughed. "What?"

They were quiet for a moment, and Milt was certain that Seth thought his husband was kidding around. Nothing much ever changed in Summitville. And teachers certainly didn't leave Summitville High midterm to hightail it off to Southern California.

When no one picked up the conversational thread, Seth wiped his mouth with a paper napkin and caught Milt's eye. "He's fucking with me, right?"

And for just a moment, the idea *did* seem absurd, a flight of fancy, something one would think of in the midst of emotional trauma, but with the passage of time would come to seem like a silly notion.

Maybe when it was time to retire he could move out there, get himself a little casita with a pool.

Milt shook his head. No. The idea wasn't the passing notion of a bereaved man. It had force. And even though Milt had yet to work out the logistics of what he knew everyone would view as a rash move, he felt deep in his gut: *I'm gonna do this.*

Milt blew out a big sigh. "If he's fucking with you, brother, I don't need to see it. If he's pulling your leg, depending on the circumstances, I might not need to see that either. But if you think your big, strapping hubby is having you on—joking with you—well, I'm afraid that's not the case." Milt looked down at the checked floor for a second, noticing the imprint of a muddy shoe, and then back up at Seth. "I'm moving to Palm Springs."

Seth shook his head, an uncertain smile creasing his face. "When?"

And Milt, even though he hadn't thought about it until right this very moment, said, "I'm putting the house on the market this week. Corky and I owned it outright, and even though the real estate market here is shit, I think our river view and our fabulous taste will see it sold quickly." Milt allowed himself only a moment to get a little choked up at the thought of their home, stripped bare of memories, inhabited by new people ready to put their own stamp on it. He knew that, later, he could grieve. Perhaps in a backyard with a lemon tree in it….

"And, as soon as I can get a moving truck together and most of the furniture sold, I'll head on out. Drive across the country. See the USA." He smiled big, trying to keep the terror at bay. A voice inside his head told him he'd scurry back here within a year, but Milt silenced it.

"C'mon," Dane said quietly. "Give yourself some time."

Milt knew his suggestion was rational, the sensible thing to do. But Milt had done the sensible thing his whole life. Maybe, just maybe, it was time to shake things up.

After all, what did he have to lose? He'd already lost the most important thing he had in this life. And, in its own harsh way, that loss allowed him the freedom to take a wild chance.

Milt put one hand on Seth's shoulder and the other on Dane's and leaned in. "The only thing I want to give myself right now is a new horizon." He smiled through his tears. "A sunny one."

CHAPTER 3

BILLY REGARDED Milt Grabaur across his dining table—a big round wooden spool he'd managed to salvage from some construction site. It was bleached by the sun and sometimes gave splinters, but it held up, year after year, in home after home, like some stalwart creature—Billy's constant companion. He'd even taken out his trailer's built-in dining table just to make room for it. There was something about how weathered it was but still strong.

It reminded Billy of himself—or maybe the man he longed to meet but could never seem to find.

They were eating Billy's homemade carnitas and tortillas. There was pico de gallo and a bowl of sour cream to tame the heat of the pork. The carnitas had a nice crust from being browned first in lard—and a mysterious sweetness from the Mexican Coke Billy used for braising.

Milt, he thought, was a ghost of a man. A haunted presence, not unlike Boo Radley in Harper Lee's *To Kill a Mockingbird.* He'd watched the man ever since he'd moved in just below him last February. At first Billy thought Milt's standoffishness could be attributed to simply settling in. Billy, who'd moved more times than he could count—which was why his own home was a rental—understood the preoccupation with building a nest for oneself. It took time and effort to take a place from being a house to a home.

Feeling a bit like a stalker, Billy found he enjoyed watching his new neighbor, even if their paths hadn't crossed in any significant way. There was something about Milt's loneliness and inherent sadness that called out to Billy. He wondered, of course, all sorts of things, like where Milt was from, how he managed to be at home every day without a job, what particular story had brought him to the desert—everyone, it seemed, had one. The valley was filled with transplants.

As time went on, Billy realized simply getting settled and making a home for himself wasn't the principle reason for his neighbor's standoffishness. No, Milt wasn't reaching out for bigger reasons, Billy decided. Ever intuitive, Billy realized this was a man who was mourning. He didn't know if the loss was of a person or a thing, but Billy picked up on the haunted look in Milt's eyes when he'd pass him walking his dog or out on his patio, reading. Billy always lofted a cheery "How you doin'?" the other man's way, hoping he'd get more in return than he did. But the best he ever got was a smile and a nod.

Billy got it. He really did. The desert was a place people often came to in hopes of starting a new life, of recreating themselves. Billy himself, just a few years ago, was one of those people. He'd come here for the sunshine, the excellent recovery community, and to

escape big-city life, which was making him feel increasingly lost and alone.

Billy had fantasized more than once that Milt
would stop in the street to chat, or that he'd invite him
onto the patio for some advice on how to best care for
the jasmine plant and the little barrel cactuses he had in
pots. Billy would advise him on watering and position-
ing for sun exposure. They'd pause—and stare mean-
ingfully into each other's eyes—then they'd proceed
inside. The dark would be cool and, at first, blinding.
The window unit would be whirring, maybe even whining as it struggled to contend with the triple-digit heat.
Barely able to see, Billy would at last get a chance to
reach out to explore the sharp planes of Milt's face with
his fingertips. Their first touch would be a charged moment, full of electricity, lust, and something else that
Billy could only imagine as coming home.

Yes, Billy had a crush.

It had developed from perhaps the first moment he
spied Milt unloading his little U-Haul truck—by himself. He wore a pair of beat-up camo cargo shorts and a
pair of hiking boots. If he'd had a shirt on, he'd wisely
gotten rid of it. His body was tight, compact, slick with
sweat. He was whiter than the average desert bear. Salt-
and-pepper hair graced not only his head and face but
also spread out in lovely curls on his broad chest. That
hair narrowed down into one of the sexiest treasure
trails Billy had ever seen (and he'd seen a few—well,
maybe more than a few), which finally disappeared into
the dark, sweat-stained waistband of his shorts. He'd
even gone over and offered to help, but Milt had merely wiped the sweat off his brow, saying only, "Thanks.
But I got it." Milt made his dismissal obvious when he
turned his back on Billy to get back to his work.

Before turning away himself, Billy allowed himself a tiny moment to savor the progress of a bead of sweat between Milt's shoulder blades as it ran, quicker, quicker, down his back and disappeared into the wonderland concealed by those damn camo shorts.

Billy worried that maybe Milt was one of the straight ones, a breeder—there were a few around, and Billy bore them no ill will. They did serve a purpose, after all.

But still, he couldn't help but admire his older neighbor, with his amazing pale gray eyes, his taut build, the way his buzzed hair clung close and thick to his perfectly formed head. Billy could imagine how all that stubble would feel between his thighs….

His bud, Kyle, back in LA, had told him, just before Billy moved out to Palm Springs, "Dude—your daddy fetish will come alive out there. Slim pickings it's not!"

Billy had to sort of mentally shake himself when he realized Milt was actually speaking. "This is delicious. Where did a Nordic type like yourself learn to cook like this?"

"Mexican boyfriend, back in Chicago. Hector. He taught me all about flavors this 'Nordic type' had no idea existed—things like cumin, oregano, bay, cilantro. Mexican food isn't about heat—it's about layers of flavor. Although I do like the shock a good habanero can bring to your tongue." Billy smiled.

Milt nodded. He looked back down at his food and picked at it.

Billy read the sadness in Milt's face. Knew it took real effort for Milt to open his mouth and compliment the food, especially when he was worried, maybe a little in shock over the events that had transpired only this afternoon.

"We're gonna find her."

"Hmm?" Milt looked up. He'd just torn off a piece of warm tortilla. Like Billy, Milt seemed to like them plain—hot with only butter and a little sprinkle of sea salt.

"You know what I'm talkin' about, Milt. Your little girl, Ruby. You'll get her back." He smiled. "I'm a little psychic. Don't scoff. I'm serious. And I'm one hundred percent certain she'll be back in your arms before the night is through."

Billy got up and looked out one of the big windows at the side of his own trailer, a silver Airstream. It was early evening, but the sky remained bright, ruthless—a dome of electric blue, showing no evidence of the clouds that had earlier brought down the storm. The little thermometer he'd mounted outside told him it was 110 degrees. Cooler than yesterday, when it got up to 120. He worried about the dog, wandering outside in the heat, with perhaps no source of water.

The rushing river that had come through their streets was now gone. If you didn't look down at the ground, Billy thought, you wouldn't even know it had rained today.

But the mud lying across the roads of the trailer park left evidence of the storm. Evidence that would take a lot of work to clean up.

It was true that Billy had always been very intuitive and maybe even a bit of an empath. But he wasn't as sure about Ruby as he let on. He didn't want Milt to worry too much, yet he couldn't help but wonder if his reassurance was a cruel thing. He hoped fate would help him out on this prediction.

He barely felt Milt come up behind him.

"I should go back."

Billy turned.

"In case she comes home," Milt added.

"You don't have to be alone. Let me clear the table and we can go out and beat the bushes for her. Okay?" Billy had to resist the urge to reach over and touch Milt's grizzled face. He still didn't know but dared to hope, anyway, what team the guy played for. Selfishly, and for only a moment, he allowed himself to regard Milt's lips, which were full, almost bow-shaped, and, Billy was certain, delectable when kissed.

"Ruby," Milt urged.

"Sure." Billy glanced back at their half-eaten meal on the table. "I'll clean this shit up later." He crossed to the fridge and grabbed a couple bottles of water. He lobbed one to Milt. "Never go out without hydration."

They started out, stepping down the rickety little steps that led down from the Airstream. Milt said, "The meal you made? That was delicious. I wish we could have finished, but all I could think about was Ruby— out there in this heat. She may be a pit bull, but she's far from tough. She's the sweetest thing." He looked away, and Billy picked up on the extra brightness in Milt's gray eyes. "I just couldn't eat, not with thinking about her out there." Milt's gaze went to the scrubland at the mountain's base.

"Let's go round her up, okay?" Billy headed out to the muddy street.

"I hope your optimism isn't unfounded."

And Billy, for the second time, felt a little shiver of doubt, even with the heat, but refused to let Milt see it. "It's not."

They searched for two hours, until the sun finally set behind the mountains. They went up and down the grid-like streets of the trailer park, asking anyone out if they'd seen her. Because of the heat, there was hardly anyone to ask. The few that *were* outside were busy trying to salvage their homes from flood damage and, understandably, weren't all that invested in Milt's canine crisis.

At least, Billy thought, it gave him a chance to introduce Milt to some of the neighbors, like the Maggios, a pair of Sicilian sisters from Milwaukee who'd never married and never lived apart. Theresa, whom everyone called Tootsie, was seventy-six, and her younger sister, Ethel, was seventy-four. They looked like twins and loved nothing more than each other and bingo. Tootsie promised to keep an eye out for the dog. "I see you walking her and can tell you already know about keeping her safe from the heat." She'd held a hand up to her forehead to shield her eyes from the sun—even though it had already gone down—and scanned the horizon. "Poor puppy." She turned back to them, and her wizened face was full of sadness and concern. Billy wanted to erase her expression for fear of scaring Milt even more. She seemed to realize the hopelessness she was displaying because she caught Milt's eyes and with a big smile said, "She's a good girl. She's gonna be okay. In fact, I bet you dollars to doughnuts, when you get back to your place, she'll be waiting for you, wondering where her supper is."

Milt thanked her and said it was nice to meet her and her sister.

"You come over sometime for a little nip of something. Maybe we could play a game of cards. You play poker?"

Milt laughed. "Badly. I'll keep that in mind."

They'd also met the young couple living next to Billy, two gay boys (almost literally—they were barely into their twenties) who'd escaped Vegas to clean up from a bad meth addiction. After they'd inquired in vain after Ruby, Billy told Milt, "I call them the sweet-and-sour twins. Cole is like some cuddly stuffed animal, wouldn't say a bad word about anyone or anything, always with a smile on his face. But Carlos is just the opposite—always grumpy, practically snarling. I worry. But somehow they seem to be happy."

"We never know what goes on in a relationship, do we?" Milt asked. They were now heading back to his trailer. "I was with my Corky for a long, long time. And some of those years, a person could look at us and think we were the happiest lovebirds alive. And then that same someone could get a gander when we were going through a rough patch—and the last several years *were* a rough patch, believe me—and feel nothing but sorrow. Still, I wouldn't trade my time with him for anything." He slowed as they approached his gate.

"Him? You said him?" Billy asked hopefully, maybe too hopefully, because it made Milt laugh.

"Yes, Billy, I'm a proud card-carrying member of the Friends of Dorothy organization."

"Me too," Billy said.

"Oh really? The rainbow flag outside and the Herb Ritts poster inside didn't give me a clue."

Billy snorted. "So, you do have a sense of humor?"

But Milt didn't join him in chuckling. After a moment he said, "Yeah, but it's been on hiatus for a while." He sighed. "And, I don't know, the gay card might be on hiatus too. Permanently."

Billy chose to pretend he didn't hear that last part.

They stopped in front of the gate to Milt's patio. The night, all around them, was still. The heat, almost suffocating, threatened to steal Billy's breath away. That's the way summer nights were in the desert—little to no relief. It was silent. Even Palm Canyon Drive, a couple of blocks over, seemed quiet for once. Billy, who never wore a watch, wondered how late it had gotten. As if the answer might be written there, he looked up at the sky, black and crowded with stars.

He was about to tell Milt that they could go to the animal shelter tomorrow. Surely someone had found Ruby and had taken her there. That's why they couldn't find her. And maybe she hadn't been microchipped, which would explain why Milt's phone hadn't rung.

The words were on Billy's lips when they heard a whimper. Billy took a step back when Milt turned to look toward the patio. There she was! Ruby emerged from underneath one of those retro metal rocking chairs. She simply sat next to the chair, tail thumping wearily against the concrete, too tired, Billy guessed, to drag herself over to her master. She whimpered again.

Or maybe it was Milt.

He rushed over to her and dropped to his knees. Sobbing, he wrapped his arms around the gray-and-white dog, burying his face in her neck.

Billy watched, not daring to interrupt. It wasn't enough that he was daddy-hot. And it wasn't enough that he was the strong, silent type. Milt was a wounded warrior—Billy could tell—and that brought out his hopelessly nurturing side.

And now—seeing the depth of emotion Milt had for his dog? Well, that clinched it.

Billy was a goner. He was in love.

God help him, because, while he knew himself, he didn't know if he'd stand a chance with this guy—and his broken heart.

Billy's own heart, though still ticking, had been to some dark places. The shadows in those places, he sometimes feared had stained him—for life. He didn't know if he had it in him to withstand the slings and arrows of that perfidious state called love.

Yet….

Billy let the happy reunion continue for a moment or so and then called out, through the dark, "You guys need to stay at my place tonight."

Milt stood up uncertainly, gaze more on the dog than Billy, as though he feared looking away from her might cause her to vanish again, and asked, "Are you sure?"

Billy rolled his eyes. "Come on. You can't stay in there. We need to get it dried out." Billy thought himself very clever for working "we" into the conversation. "I know my place is tiny, but you and Ruby can have my bed and I'll surf the couch. She like carnitas?"

"She likes everything, especially if there's meat involved."

Girl, you and I have something in common. I like meat too. Billy eyed Ruby, then gave Milt the once-over. *Large quantities of meat.*

Dog by his side, Milt came toward him. "If you're sure we won't be a bother…."

Billy rolled his eyes. "I wouldn't have offered otherwise. That's what we do at Summer Winds. Help our neighbors out."

Billy stared into Milt's face and wasn't sure if he saw guilt or gratitude there.

CHAPTER 4

THE CELL door slammed shut with a clang. The sound made Billy think of endings, final moments, points of no return. The clang was an echo that called out in the dark, "No tomorrow." He watched as the guard walked away, whistling, not looking back.

"Dude. Hey, dude. You know what time it is?"

Billy looked over his shoulder at the man sharing the cell with him. Most people, Billy thought, would look at this guy and think "gangbanger," but Billy could see beyond the neck tattoo and the black-and-white skull bandana, the baggy jeans and the tight white T-shirt and see a scared kid. He couldn't have been more than twenty. Billy moved away from the bars to sit down on the cot opposite.

"What's your name?" Billy asked.

"The fuck? I only asked if you knew the time, man."

Billy smiled, leaning forward to peer more deeply into the boy's dark, dark eyes. "What's your name?"

"Jorge." Billy noticed the way he rolled the *r* in his name; there was a lilt there. Spanish was probably his first language.

"Billy." He stared grimly around the little cell, taking in its bleak lack of color, its antiseptic smell covering up God knew what. A cockroach skittered across the floor, through the bars, and out of sight. Ah, sweet freedom. Even a cockroach was better off….

"So?" Jorge leaned a little forward, the metal chain securing his wallet clanking a little. "The time? You got it?"

Billy actually looked down at his wrist. But he hadn't had a watch since a trick had swiped it one night down at Steamworks, the bathhouse in Boystown. That had been—what—a year ago now.

"I don't know, Jorge. You got someplace to be? A hot date?"

That made Jorge chuckle.

"I would imagine it's the wee small hours of the morning, like the song says."

Jorge didn't register any recognition of the song title. Billy would have been surprised if he did. "When I got picked up, the bar I was coming out of was closing. They have a 2:00 a.m. license." Billy stared up at the water-stained ceiling, figuring. "With the trip here in the car, booking, and so on and so forth, I'd guess it's going on four now. Maybe even five." He eyed Jorge. "Will your mama be worried?"

The little smile that had flickered around Jorge's full lips vanished. "Shut up, man. You don't know nothin'." He lay down on his cot, drawing his knees up to his chest, away from Billy. He was skin and bones, and it made Billy, even in this fucked-up, inebriated state, want to take care of him—not in a lecherous way but as a father might, even though he was far too old to be his son.

The boy, after a moment, began snoring softly. Other than that it had grown quiet. Somewhere, one of the cops was talking on the phone, arguing with a girlfriend, Billy guessed, because of the many "baby, babies" he used and the oft-voiced refrain, "You just don't understand."

The wee small hours…. Billy turned the words over and over in his mind as he lay on his back, hands behind his head. He'd sung the song earlier that night to a drunken crowd at a little bar called Roosters, on Western Avenue in the far north neighborhood of Rogers Park. Billy had just been hired to play the piano and sing, his first gig in more than three months, and he'd started off last night, a Monday, with optimism. He'd done covers of Coldplay songs, Ed Sheeran, even a little K.D. Lang, never reaching too far back in time to confuse the sparse—and thirtysomething—patrons.

He'd started off with Billy Joel's "Piano Man," and the self-reference made him maudlin. And when Billy got maudlin, he got drunk. A misguided lass, called herself Betsy, with dark hair, darker eyes, and a zaftig body, had sent him numerous bourbon and Cokes when she found out that was his poison of choice, drawing her chair near Billy's upright piano as though staking her claim. In her blowsy muslin top, heavy silver jewelry, and fashionably distressed jeans, she gave off an air of desperation that reduced her somehow. Even if Billy had been straight, he thought he would have been put off by her. But she was generous with the drinks….

After he'd loosened up with three or four cocktails, and Betsy had moved close enough to place a possessive hand on his jean-clad knee, Billy had looked at her, smiling, and said, "Sugar, you're sweet."

Her smile widened.

"But I am as gay as a picnic basket." He played a few chords of "I Will Survive."

Betsy, smile gone, didn't get the reference. She withdrew her hand as if he'd told her he had leprosy. Or AIDS.

Billy continued playing the gay anthem in a slow, plodding way—making it almost a melancholy tune, a dirge. "So, if you were hoping maybe we'd hook up later tonight, once I finished up my starring appearance here at this fine establishment, you'd be barking up the wrong tree. Woof! Woof!" He realized he was speaking too loud and too precisely—a sign he was getting quickly to the point of being overserved—and snickered. He took his hands off the keys and jerked a thumb at his chest. "This boy here—he prefers sausage over pie, if you get my drift."

Betsy's warm features flattened, going all thin and horizontal. She stood up. "I was just trying to be nice to you," she hissed. "I don't care what you like!"

She started away. *Oh, sister, but you do. You really do.* As she walked away, Billy launched into Irving Berlin's "What'll I Do?" and sang it out, too loud and a little off-key, not that anyone would notice in this joint. Half the laminate tables were empty. The other half were filled with middle-aged men, hoping for a gal just like Betsy. Billy was confident she'd find her Mr. Right, or at least Right Now, tonight.

He stopped midway through "What'll I Do?" and, for Betsy, launched into "Someday My Prince Will Come." He couldn't sing because he was snickering and eyeing Betsy, who was on a stool at the bar, doing her best to shoot daggers with her eyes.

With the fog in his brain, Billy did have the presence of mind to chastise himself. *You're being mean. She didn't do anything to you other than show some interest.*

The shame Billy felt made his face hot.

Even though Betsy no longer plied him with drinks, the bartender, a cute bearded redhead, was only too happy to make sure his cocktail glass remained full. By the end of the night, Billy was hopelessly drunk and could no longer find any melody hidden among the black-and-whites. He could barely sit upright.

When the lights came up and the few patrons left stumbled outside to find cabs, or God forbid, drive themselves home, Billy was hunched over the piano, just about asleep. A line of drool ran from his lower lip to the keys.

The ginger bartender reached under Billy's armpits and lifted gently. "C'mon, buddy. You need to get yourself home."

Billy leaned back into the bartender's chest, still aware enough to notice the firm pecs under the Cubbies T-shirt. He stumbled a little, but with the bartender's help managed to stand upright, as long as he held on to the edge of the piano for support.

"You want me to call you a cab?"

"No. I want you to call me lover boy." Billy smiled.

The bartender did not. He looked away from Billy as though he were something he'd scrape off the bottom of his shoe.

Billy's anger rose, sudden, a horde of bees buzzing inside his head. "Hey, don't look at me like that. You're the one that kept sending me drinks all night."

The bartender—and his name, Kenton, came to Billy suddenly—smiled. "And I was the one that forced you to drink them? Held a gun to your head?"

Billy, who when sober might have had a snappier comeback, simply stared at Kenton, swaying a little. After a moment he said, almost too softly for his own ears, "Yeah, could you call me a cab?"

Kenton shook his head. Billy realized the point of relying on this guy for kindness was past. "I can call you what you are—a talentless drunk."

"That's not very nice." Billy sat down suddenly and hard on the piano stool. "How about one for the road, then?"

"Get out of here, man. And don't come back."

"Seriously?" Billy asked. "And on whose authority do you speak?"

"Mine. See, I not only bartend, I own this joint." He groped in his pocket and pulled out a few crumpled twenties. He put them in Billy's hand and then closed Billy's fingers over them. "There's enough there to get yourself home and whatever you think you 'earned' here tonight."

"Fuck you." Billy tucked the bills into his pocket. He wasn't drunk enough to forget that, between his behavior and the cost of all the bourbon he'd guzzled, he was lucky the guy didn't ask *him* for money.

He started toward the door, taking very slow and deliberate steps. He paused to ask, over his shoulder, "You got a smoke?"

"Go on. On your way." The bartender made a little dismissive walking gesture with his fingers.

Billy paused at the door. He wasn't sure why. Maybe he was trying to figure who had hired him over the weekend—it sure as hell wasn't this guy. Some big gal in a black-and-white checkered dress and sensible black flats had proclaimed him "wonderful" and told him he was "too good for the likes of this joint, but we won't look a gift horse in the mouth."

Billy sighed and pushed the door open. Everything he touched turned to shit.

The bartender called, "Get some help, Billy. Really. You have talent."

Billy looked over his shoulder, but Kenton had turned his back as he slid into a denim jacket. Maybe the words Billy had just heard were nothing more than wishful thinking. After all, only moments ago, the guy had said he had *no* talent. *Pick a lane, asshole.*

Outside, the sparse traffic on Western seemed dizzying to Billy, and he leaned against a lamppost while figuring that, if he just walked to the bus stop up the street, he could grab a bus home to his roach-infested studio on Howard Avenue and save the money he'd otherwise use on cab fare. That damn bus stop, though, looked *so* far away. And he felt like he was going to be sick….

He never got to the bus stop. Nor did he get home.

Now, in this cell, while Jorge snored his confinement away, Billy realized the last thing he remembered was leaning against the lamppost. The next thing he knew, he was in jail.

He'd had a couple of blackouts before, but he'd always managed somehow—by the grace of God—to get himself home, to his own bed.

He began to shiver. He didn't know if he was cold or on the brink of quitting drinking, one way or another. Because he knew he'd been playing this game too long—the drinking, the drugging, the promiscuity. *You only have so many chances before the game's over. You*

*can win or you can lose. And with the path you're on,
buddy boy, you might not even get to make that choice.
The drink might get you. The coke or the crystal might
get you. Or even one of those hot tricks, who never
seem so hot once the deed is done and you're watching them walk away with your wallet in their pocket,
might decide to end the game—just for kicks. Sobering
thoughts....* At this last, Billy couldn't help but chuckle
bitterly at the pun.

With fear, self-loathing, and shame for company,
Billy Blue joined his cellmate in slumber.

He awoke with no idea how much time had passed,
but with knowledge of two things—the side of his face
was caked in dried vomit that had an acidic stink, and
a new guard, this one an African American guy with
round wire-rim glasses and a build like a defensive
tackle, was standing outside his cell.

His stare told Billy all he needed to know. It was
like the guy had just sucked on a lemon.

"Get up. You got bail. Your neighbor's here."

Billy sat up. A sharp stab of pain, like a blade behind his eyes, made him wince and suck in a breath. He
angrily wiped at the crusty upchuck on his cheek until
all he could feel was skin and stubble. The room spun,
his stomach churned, and he was afraid he might puke
again.

"What?" Billy barely knew his neighbors. The best
he could say was that he had a nodding acquaintance
with a few of them.

"Dude. You're out. I don't have time to tell you
a story." The guard opened the door and stood there,
waiting. "Coming? I need to lock up behind you."

Billy stood on the legs of a newborn fawn and
looked around. There was a sink in the corner, and with

a "Hang on a sec" to the guard, he rinsed his face. He doubted he looked much better, but at least he smelled a tiny bit fresher.

In the booking area, he spied his neighbor sitting on a bench by the front door. He didn't know the guy's name but recognized him from the courtyard of the white brick apartment building where they both lived. He was an older man, tall and thin, with an overall effect of washed-out gray. His skin was sallow, his head almost bald save for a few gray whiskers around the pate. His ears stuck out almost comically. He wore a pair of chino work pants, dark blue, and a button-down white shirt, dingy and frayed around the collar and cuffs but clean. His feet were the only thing that had any color, and that's why Billy's gaze was immediately drawn to them. Red Cons.

Billy smiled when their eyes met, and the corners of the guy's lips lifted in a world-weary grin. Billy immediately thought the smile looked like something a father might dish out to a kid to whom he'd already given one too many second chances. Kind, yet guarded, self-protective.

The guard had him sign some paperwork and patted him on the arm to let him know he was free to go.

Billy approached the guy cautiously. As he did, the man stood. Billy noticed he held a baseball cap in his hands, and he twirled the cap restlessly. The hands were wizened, callused, the tools of a working man.

Billy wished he knew his name, wished he'd taken a moment to ask for this simple identifier from a neighbor who he now recalled had always been friendly. But Billy was forever wrapped up in his own little journey of self-destruction and had no time for others unless they had drugs, booze, or sex to offer up.

"Billy?"

Billy closed his eyes for a second. *Oh shit, he knows my name. Who* is *this guy? My guardian angel?*

Billy grinned. Once upon a time, a smile was all he needed to dazzle a stranger—to open doors. Charm the pants off gullible boys. Cause folks to pull the lever to cast a vote of confidence.

Billy didn't put much stock in his smile these days. He'd looked in a mirror. What stared back—a haggard guy looking much older than his midtwenties—frightened him. The whites of his eyes were tarnished by broken red veins.

"Yeah," Billy answered. He scratched as his neck, the skin feeling oily and gritty. "Did you, um, did you bail me out?" He cocked his head.

The guy nodded. "Yup."

"Why would you do that? You don't even know me." Billy wished he could reel the words back in. They seemed both ungrateful and cruel.

The man gave him a broad smile, revealing very even white teeth. Dentures?

"I know you better than you think." He chuckled. "I'm a busybody. Jimmy Stewart in *Rear Window* minus the crutches and Grace Kelly. I keep an eye on my neighbors. You're one of the more interesting ones."

"Oh?"

"Yeah." The guy turned to look out through the double plate glass doors a few steps down from where they stood. "You want to go outside? This place gives me the creeps." He winked. "Bad memories."

Wordlessly, Billy followed him out the door. Morning had managed to rise, despite Billy's troubles, and it was already hot and humid as only a summer day in Chicago can be. The sky above was not a pretty shade of blue but a dirty white bowl turned upside down. The sun was a feeble yet paradoxically intense sphere of paler white to the east. The air was heavy with exhaust fumes. Trash lay in the gutters.

Billy felt light-headed, a little dizzy. He wanted two things—a drink and a cigarette. But he didn't dare ask this guy for either. After all, he'd done enough already. But Billy *did* need to know who his savior was this particular summer morning.

"I don't mean to be rude," Billy said, "But you have me at a disadvantage. You know my name. And I'm embarrassed to admit I don't know yours."

"Jon. Jon McGregor. I live on the fourth floor, facing the courtyard."

"Sorry, I must have forgotten."

Jon shook his head. "No, you didn't forget. You never asked." Jon didn't seem accusatory when he said this—just stating a fact.

Still, Billy felt a little rush of shame.

"Thank you for coming down here and bailing me out. How did you even know I was in jail?"

Jon took a moment to answer. From his pocket he withdrew a pack of Marlboro Reds and a black disposable lighter. Billy wanted to drop to his knees in gratitude when he offered the pack. Trying not to appear too eager, Billy grabbed a smoke and the lighter and lit up. "Thanks," he said, exhaling a blue cloud that hung motionless in the moist air.

"Welcome." Jon lit up, blew the smoke away from Billy's face. "For both."

"So, how did you know?"

"Let's go for a little walk," Jon said, turning and beginning to walk north. "I know a place that serves a mean cup of joe. You look like you could use a pick-me-up."

What I could use is a shot and beer. An eye-opener, as my dad used to say. "Okay." Billy fell into step alongside Jon.

They walked in silence, smoking, until Billy could take it no longer. "But seriously, man, how did you know I was in jail? And why on earth would you want to bail me out?" The words "There's no way I can pay you back" were already on his lips before he snatched them back, recognizing them for how worthless they were.

Jon stopped, turned to Billy. "I caught your set last night." He grinned. "Started out good. Real good. You remind me a little of Boz Scaggs." He chuckled. "You probably don't even know who he is."

"Before my time, but sure I do. I've been known to sing 'We're All Alone' inspired by him. And thank you—old Boz has a great voice and some style."

"Good song. Rita Coolidge does it better, but I'd like to hear your take sometime." Jon stared out at the street, finishing his smoke. "As I said, you started out good, but then—"

"The drinking got the better of me," Billy interrupted him before he could say words to that effect.

Jon nodded. "That's putting it mildly."

"And to add another question to the pile, how did you even know I was singing? At Roosters, for Christ's sake?" In his mind's eye, Billy pictured the front of the sad little dive, with its blacked-out front window and its flashing neon Old Style beer sign.

Jon laughed. "You told me. Friday morning. We passed in the courtyard. Invited me to come out and see your Rogers Park debut."

Billy scratched his head.

"You don't remember, do you?"

"Not a clue." Billy didn't have even the slightest recollection of the encounter, which made him wonder what else he'd forgotten, what events just slipped below the psychic surface without a ripple.

"I was lugging, like, four bags from Jewel. Wore a diamond tiara and had a white gardenia behind my ear. Smoking a cigar. Clown shoes?"

Billy laughed and shook his head. "Friday morning's a bit of a blur."

Jon clasped Billy's shoulder for a moment. "It's okay."

"Funny. I don't remember how I got *here*, either." Billy felt a sudden urge to burst into tears. He took a big breath to hold things at bay.

"I followed you out of the bar because you weren't too steady on your feet. I tend to worry. Didn't want to see you get run down by a bus." Jon took a drag off his cigarette. "You passed out on the ground. Fell as only a drunk can—somehow managing not to hurt yourself, sort of bounced. I tried to get you up, called 911 when you told me you were fine there on the sidewalk."

Billy felt a rush of disgust for himself. "I said that?"

Jon nodded. "Cops came, brought you in. I could have followed the blue-and-white but figured you could use a little time in the slammer to sober up." He smiled, and this time it was kind. "I know from experience what that's like."

"So, what? You just decided to be a Good Samaritan? Come down and bail me out 'cause you had nothing better to do with your money?"

"Actually, yes."

"I'll pay you back." Billy had no idea how, though. He was behind in his electricity and his rent.

"No, you won't, so please don't say it. I didn't fork out bail because I thought it was a loan. Look at it as an investment in your future." Jon's gaze forced Billy to look him in the eye. "You can pay me back by paying it forward, as they say."

"Why would you do this?" It hurt Billy's heart to accept this kindness, especially from a man he barely knew. It didn't feel like the guy had strings attached, but who knew?

Jon laughed. "Ah. It's not much. Don't overthink it. Try to have an attitude of gratitude, okay? Just be open to receive."

Billy nodded. "Well, why the hell not?" He still didn't feel right about this. Maybe it was because he felt, deep down, he didn't deserve to be treated with kindness. He turned and looked up, realizing they stood in front of a Catholic church. It looked old, a marriage of fieldstone, wood, and stained glass, its spire rising up toward the skim-milk sky. A broad expanse of concrete steps led to the heavy wood-and-metal double doors.

"You said you knew a place for coffee?" Billy asked, wanting to flee the house of worship.

Jon nodded at the church front doors. "Right here. Good old Saint Augustine's."

Billy scratched his head. "For coffee?"

Jon smiled. "It's made with holy water. Goes great with a side of communion wafers."

"Really?"

"No, dumbass. There's a meeting here in—" Jon glanced down at his watch, a Timex that looked like it had taken more than a few lickin's. "—about ten minutes."

"A meeting?"

"What are you, a mynah bird?"

Billy shook his head, looked away. When had he finished the cigarette Jon had given him? When could he ask for another? The thought popped into his head that Saint Augustine was the one who said something like "Lord, give me chastity—but not yet." Not that the quote had anything to do with anything.

Or maybe it did and Billy didn't want to face it.

Billy felt something very close to dread. "When you say a meeting—"

Jon cut him off. "Yes, Billy, I've brought you to an AA meeting. Have you never been to one before?"

"No, no, of course not. Why would I? And I'm not sure I need one now." Billy felt the anger build inside, the urge to simply turn on his heel and run. Who knew where? Billy knew—the closest local bar open at this hour of the morning. He sighed.

"The meeting's a suggestion, Billy. You're a grown man. You can do what you want." As though Jon had read his mind, he said, "There's an Irish pub two blocks south and around the corner. Would you rather go there? You're a free man in paradise." Jon's eyes probed.

Billy felt heat rise to his face. Caught. He hung his head so he could better observe the cast-off Popeyes box at his feet.

He heard Jon talking. "Look. Just come in and listen. You don't have to say a word. You don't have to do a thing. Just hear what people say, their stories. If you want what's on offer, then great. If not, I'll stand you to a beer at O'Malley's."

"You're a weird guy, you know that?" Billy found it hard to swallow over the lump in his throat.

"You won't be the first to call me weird, friend, and I'm pretty sure you won't be the last. I'll take it as a compliment."

Billy started up the steps to the church front doors. It was the least he could do, after the mystifying lengths this character had gone to for him. How long did an AA meeting last, anyway? An hour? Billy shrugged. As he opened the door for Jon, he asked, "You think I'm an alcoholic?"

"I think what *I* think doesn't matter. I also think you know the answer to that question." Jon smirked. He leaned in as they entered the church and whispered, "Just keep your mind open, okay?"

And Billy promised he would.

CHAPTER 5

"I CAN'T take your bed." Milt looked nervously around the interior of the trailer as though there might be other beds he'd missed that he and Ruby could use for the night. Or would it be for more than the night? How long would it take for his trailer to dry out? To replace the essentials that needed replacing?

Billy tucked in the bottom half of a clean set of sheets. They were light blue, like Billy's eyes, and smelled of fabric softener. Milt was glad they'd taken the time to give Ruby a little cleanup before bringing her inside. Was there anything more comforting than the smell of clean sheets? Milt was so tired that he could fall headfirst into that expanse of blue cotton before him and simply sleep for days. The sheets almost called out to him, beckoning. *Why am I so hesitant to accept this gift?*

Maybe it was because he didn't know this Billy person. Not really. It didn't seem right to accept *too* much hospitality from someone he'd just met. Milt would do just fine, wouldn't he, huddled up on the little love seat behind him? It wouldn't be too uncomfortable if he dangled his legs over the edge….

Billy unfurled the top sheet in the air with a snapping noise that sounded like the crack of a whip. Ruby eyed him and slowly, cautiously, backed behind the beat-up corduroy recliner. After a second she poked her head out, regarding both men with intense dark eyes.

"You can sleep in the bed, and you will. I don't want to hear any more about it." Billy tucked in the top sheet, threw a worn but beautiful patchwork quilt in shades of teal, orange, and gray overtop, and then added a couple of pillows. Looking pleased with himself, he placed his hands on his hips and said, "Looks pretty comfy, huh?"

"Yes, yes it does." Milt sighed. "Are you sure? Where will you sleep?" Milt eyed the love seat as though it were a torture device. And, for a big guy like Billy, he was certain it would be.

"I have a sleeping bag. I'll be fine on the floor." He leaned in close, and Milt was almost breathless at the sight of the purity of his face—the clean, unlined skin, so smooth. He wondered what it would feel like to run his fingers across Billy's cheekbones, along his jaw, to tease the cleft in his chin.

Stop it now! He's just a boy. A neighbor trying to help you out. Milt felt heat rise to his face that he recognized as shame. "Are you sure?"

"Please. Will you stop? I'm *not* going to debate this with you, no matter how hard you try. You've been through a hell of an ordeal today. You're exhausted. I don't mean to be rude, but it shows. I can say the same for Ruby over there, hiding behind the chair. And I don't mind if she joins you on the bed."

Milt had to bite his tongue not to say, "I wouldn't mind if *you* joined me on the bed." But he knew how lecherous that would sound, how creepy. And besides, it could only be a platonic invitation anyway.

You made a promise.

Milt looked outside and saw that it was just beginning to get dark. One thing he loved about the desert was how inky the sky was and how the stars sparkled more brightly here, how each of them stood out more prominently. For the first time, Milt could easily make out constellations, trace the course of a falling star, see the Milky Way. He always imagined one of the stars was his Corky, looking down on him, keeping him safe.

Lord, what must he think seeing me now, with this young buck? Milt laughed.

"What's so funny?"

Milt replied, "Nothin'. Just a thought. Hey, at least let me go grab a bottle of wine. A little rain couldn't have hurt my wine rack, right? I got some nice reds. You like wine, Billy? Or I have beer too."

Billy turned from Milt to fluff the pillows. "I'm fine, Milt. The only thing you need to do is get some shut-eye. Okay?"

Milt sat down on the edge of the bed. Tail between her legs, Ruby came over to sit beside him. He scratched her behind the ears, feeling an almost heart-wrenching burst of love and gratitude that she wasn't lost to the storm. "Okay, but tomorrow I'm taking you out for breakfast, anywhere you want. And we can also figure out where I can stay until we get my home back in order."

"You can stay here, Milt."

"No. It's too much." *And too tempting.* "No offense, buddy, but you don't have a lot of space to spare."

Billy laughed. "Well, I can't argue with that, but seriously, you're welcome here."

"I appreciate that."

After a period of silence that went on just long enough to become awkward, Billy stretched and said, "I'm gonna take a little walk, let you guys get settled. I can stop in at your place if you want me to grab anything. I promise to be quiet when I get home."

Milt couldn't think of anything he needed, at least, nothing he couldn't get for himself in the morning. "I'm good. And don't worry about waking us up. It's your house."

"Be it ever so humble."

"It's nice! And I, for one, really appreciate staying here. And so does Ruby." Milt flopped back on the bed and suddenly feared he might be asleep before Billy opened the door to step out into the night. He stared up at the plain white ceiling, imagining stars suspended there. His eyelids fluttered and he yawned.

He barely heard Billy leave. Ruby hopped up on the bed, circled, and then lay down between his legs, which barely registered.

Milt was asleep in no time.

HE AND Corky were driving one of Summitville's winding hilly roads. Trees, their leaves green, lined the roadway, and Milt was comfortable in the passenger seat but alert, watching the road as Corky maneuvered the hairpin turns and the rises and descents of their journey.

Corky looked sure of himself—vision clear, gaze only leaving the road for a second or two here and there to look over at Milt and smile.

"You're back?" Milt asked.

"Back from where?"

"I don't know, wherever it was you went."

"Never really left. It was you who checked out."

Milt bristled a bit in spite of his happiness at being reunited with Corky. "Honey, I never went anywhere. I was with you until the very last second."

Corky glanced over. "There is no last second."

Milt thought that one over. He watched as the car floated a bit as they rounded a particularly tight downhill curve. The out-of-control sensation, the car's wheels leaving the road, caused a feeling of giddy delight to rise up in Milt rather than panic.

Corky looked unconcerned, a small lopsided smile creasing his features.

And then they were crashing through brush at the side of the road.

And then they were flying off the edge of a cliff.

Airborne.

But Milt felt no worries, no fears about crashing down onto solid ground below, the impact more than jarring and most likely fatal.

There was freedom in this flight. Faith in knowing that Corky was driving.

And all would be well.

MILT DIDN'T come awake with a start. It was simply this—one moment he slept, dreaming, and the next he was wide-awake. He reached up to feel tears on his face. Despite them, he didn't feel sad.

For a moment he was a little disoriented, looking first toward where a window should be and now where there was only a smooth wall. He shook his head a little, turned over on his back. The reality of the day before swept in, the flood, the kindness of Billy, practically passing out here on Billy's bed.

The trailer was still, save for the easy snores of not one, but two creatures nearby. Milt smiled. The symphony of snores and whimpers wasn't annoying. Instead, it was oddly comforting, nearly lulling him back to sleep.

But his dream was still there, in his consciousness. Still vivid. That sensation of flying over land and a body of water—maybe the Ohio River—in a vehicle he now recognized as the Kia Optima they'd once owned before they got the Mazda SUV. What should have been terrifying, because as Milt knew, what went up must come down, was not. No, he felt a certain comfort with his dead husband at the wheel, a certain feeling he could lean into and rely on—all would be well.

He smiled. There was no need to ponder the meaning of the dream.

Ruby snuggled closer, and he lifted his arm to accommodate her.

From the floor there was the sound of a long and hornlike fart. Milt laughed; he couldn't help himself.

A disembodied voice floated up. "Sorry."

"Don't worry about it," Milt said.

"You awake?"

"Clearly."

"I recommend no deep breathing for a couple of minutes."

"Noted." Milt laughed again.

"Was that what woke you up?"

"What? Your flatulence? No." Milt rolled over on his side. He scooted toward the edge of the bed, where he could see Billy lying on the floor. Billy had thrown back the top of the sleeping bag and lay, legs apart, arms behind

head, clad only in a pair of tighty-whities. The view, Milt
had to admit, was breathtaking, enhanced rather than ob-
scured by the rays of silver moonlight bathing him. He
went on, "I had a weird dream. Well, not so much weird
as...." Milt's voice trailed off as he searched for the right
word. "Memorable," he came up with at last.

"Oh?" Billy asked. He rolled over on his stomach,
with his chin propped up by his hands.

That view is too much! Milt turned over on his
back, debating whether he should share this very personal dream—and his interpretation of it—with someone, really, he barely knew, despite being in his bed.
*Why not? It's not like he's going to judge. And talking
about it might help cement it in my mind.*

Milt began, staring up at the ceiling instead of
looking at Billy. "My late husband, Corky, and I were
driving." And he went on to describe the details of the
dream, particularly the odd sensation of flying in a vehicle high above the ground and the fact that he felt no
fear.

"You felt safe," Billy said from the floor.

"Exactly. Not just safe, but shepherded in a way."

"Shepherded?"

"Yeah, like I was being led, being taken care of,
like the reins, or the steering wheel in this case, were
out of my hands, but I had no worries because I could
trust Corky. He was taking care of me—from beyond."
Uttering those words was a tremendous comfort for
Milt, making him feel wrapped in something warm and
fleecy.

Billy didn't say anything for a long time, so long
that Milt began to wonder if he'd fallen back asleep.

"He really loved you," Billy said, voice soft as velvet, from out of the dark.

"He did. I spent pretty much my whole adult life with him."

"He must have. To visit you like that, to let you know he was keeping an eye on you, on things, making sure everything was safe."

Milt had his mouth open to respond and then shut it. One word Billy had said sunk in—"visit." *No, it was only a dream, a way for my subconscious to conjure up some comfort from my own tragedy.*

And yet, with a heart-certainty, Milt felt Billy was right. It *was* a visit. He could still see Corky in the car beside him—his alert eyes and his smile, things that had gone missing over his horrible decline. In a weird way, Milt still felt him, right next to him. There was a sense of both endings and beginnings.

If it truly was a visit, Milt was certain this experience, this winged drive, would never fade as dreams do.

"Thanks for that," he whispered, his breath stolen by emotion.

But Billy had already fallen asleep. Or at least he didn't answer.

CHAPTER 6

MYRON'S CAFÉ in Cathedral City was a mis-
named little diner in a strip mall. God only knew why
it wasn't called Marilyn's, or maybe Some Like It Hot,
or even Norma Jean's. The reason? The place wasn't
just decorated, it was *festooned* with portraits of Marilyn Monroe throughout her life—big black-and-white
framed posters, movie stills, even a shelf that ran just
below the ceiling around almost the whole diner displaying Franklin Mint plates bearing images of the star.
Billy always felt this restaurant could only happen in
the Palm Springs area, where streets were named for
movie stars. Bob Hope, Dinah Shore, Frank Sinatra,
Kirk Douglas, and others had become more than stars
to Billy—these days he thought of them more often as
ways to get someplace.

After they got to the hostess desk, Billy turned to
gauge Milt's reaction. "Don't tell me you've already
been?"

"No, no. I think I'd remember." Milt grinned, his gaze roving over all the iconic images. "I've never seen a place like this. Sure didn't have anything like it back home. It's like stepping into a Marilyn Monroe museum. Is the food any good? Don't tell me they have cutesy names for the dishes. Gentlemen Prefer Pancakes, maybe?"

Billy shook his head as Milt snickered. Before he could respond, the hostess, a seventy-something woman who could have been Marilyn herself, with her upsweep of platinum hair and heavy eyeliner, welcomed them. Her name tag read Trixie. She led them to a booth in the back and handed them each a menu.

After they had their coffee and were waiting for their breakfasts (which did *not* have cutesy names)—corned beef hash and poached eggs for Milt, blueberry pancakes and bacon for Billy—Billy asked Milt, "So why don't you ever talk to anybody? Not to be confrontational, but most folks make a *little* effort to meet their neighbors."

Billy wanted to pause and hit rewind on the words. He watched as Milt's face reddened and his smile vanished. Milt looked down at the Plexiglas tabletop, beneath which were ads for local businesses, as though he were searching desperately for a plumber or new nightclub hangout.

"Ah, damn it, man. I'm sorry. I have a way about me that often ends with my foot in my mouth. Too blunt by half. Never mind. Let's talk about something else."

Milt didn't say anything for a long while. Long enough, in fact, that Billy began to be worried that this would be like one of those painful first dates, where pulling a word out of your partner was almost impossible. Long enough that Billy began to fear an offended

Milt might simply get up from the table and walk home. It was a bit of a hike, but still only three miles or so, so the trek wouldn't be out of the question.

And Billy wouldn't blame him.

But then Trixie arrived, balancing their plates artfully. She set them down correctly, refilled coffee mugs. "Everything look okay? Get you anything else? Hot sauce?"

If Trixie was wise to the tension hanging just above the surface of the table—Billy visualized it as a noxious black cloud—she didn't say anything. Her smile didn't even waver. When neither asked for hot sauce, card tricks, or for Trixie to stand on her head, she left.

Billy got busy drowning his pancakes in syrup, knowing he'd need to ask for more. Sugar, in any form, was one indulgence he allowed himself these days. He wasn't sure he actually heard Milt speak when he did, or if his mind was playing wishful thinking tricks on him.

"It's a fair question."

Billy looked up and met Milt's gaze. Milt was busy buttering his toast. When he glanced up, he smiled at Billy. "Yeah, fair. You live right behind me, probably have been seeing me every day. It's only natural to wonder."

Yeah. I noticed you from the very start. I wanted to get to know you—badly. I hoped and hoped and hoped for—one, a sign that you were gay, and two, a sign that you might be interested in me. I was disappointed every single fucking time.

Milt went on. "And you're right, hard as it is for me to hear it. Most folks, when they land in a new place, want to meet the people who live around them. They want to get to know their neighbors. It's normal. And

maybe I'm one of those folks who's just not—normal."
He snickered. "Ha! If you only knew…."

Billy still felt bad. "You shouldn't feel any need to
explain yourself to me."

Milt chewed, swallowed. "And yet I do. Feel com-
pelled. I want you to know me. I want to know you. So
yeah, I haven't been the most outgoing neighbor. I hav-
en't wanted to reach out. To paraphrase Greta Garbo, I
wanted to be alone."

Milt looked away for a moment. "Corky dying
shook me to my core."

Billy couldn't help it. He felt a paradoxical mix
of sympathy and a baser instinct, one he wasn't proud
of—jealousy. Just a twinge, but it was there. He tried
to swallow the lower of his two impulses. He reached
out and covered Milt's hand with his own, forced Milt
to meet his gaze.

After a moment Milt looked away, moved his hand,
and got busy with his food. As he cut up his eggs and
then mixed them in with the hash, he talked. "Corky was
gone, in a way, long before that final hour when he drew
his last breath. Alzheimer's is rough—especially on the
ones who are left to pick up the pieces. It sounds awful
to say this, but Corky was pretty much unaware of any
pain or embarrassment toward the end. He was too out of
it. In his own little world. But I suffered. I remembered
my strong man. The guy who did the *New York Times*
crossword puzzle in ink on a Sunday morning. The one
who could make me feel safe from any ill the world had
to offer just by wrapping his arms around me."

Billy felt the twinge of jealousy again, like something cutting into his heart. He hated himself for it, because here was a fellow human being taking a chance
and pouring out his grief, and he was making it all

about himself. Still, jealousy wasn't an emotion one controlled, and it certainly wasn't something that had any logic. By its very nature, jealousy was selfish.

"That's so sweet. You must have a big heart, Milt."

Milt waved the compliment away. "Bigger than the Grinch's, anyway. Before it grew. But I'd actually like to think my heart's the same size as everyone else's. I'd like to think everything I did for the man I love is what anyone would do if they were in my shoes and really cared about the person they shared their lives with." Milt looked up from his food and at Billy. "Wouldn't you?"

The question caught him off guard. Would he? He'd like to think that of course he would. Most of us want to believe that when the chips were down, we'd rise up to be our highest and best selves. But Billy suddenly felt very young. He hadn't been called upon to take care of someone else as Milt had.

"I'd like to believe I would," Billy said, and he confessed to Milt that he'd never been put in a position where he was responsible for someone's life.

Milt cocked his head. "Not even your own?"

Wow. Billy thought for a moment. It seemed to be his morning for being caught short by personal questions. All he'd wanted to do was introduce his neighbor to a place he thought was cool. Himself? The question actually chilled him more than the air-conditioning in this joint, which was working its figurative fingers to the bone to beat the three-digit temperature outside. Billy said quietly, "Yeah. There's a history of that. But I don't want to talk about it right now."

Why's it so hard to get to know another human being? Why do we have to make ourselves so vulnerable? Why can't we just skip ahead to something warm and comfortable like a pair of old fleece-lined slippers?

God make me patient—right now. Billy snorted with laughter at his last thought.

"What?"

"Nothin'. Tell me about Corky."

And Milt did. He went on and on, regaling Billy with how they'd met—in a bar when they were both on vacation in Chicago. A leather bar, of all things, that wasn't there anymore, called the Cell Block, on Halsted. His face reddened as he spoke about their first meeting, and Billy caught on that was because they'd hooked up in the bar's dark back room. For shame! He talked about their love of travel, how Kauai was a favorite Hawaiian island, how they both adored Rome over almost any other place on the planet, how they never got to see their dream of an Alaskan cruise realized. He told of lazy nights making spaghetti, of summer days sunning on the pebbled banks of the Ohio River, of birthdays and Christmases together, of their shared desire for a kid that never came true, despite a real attempt to adopt. And logically, of the parade of much-loved and spoiled mutts that passed through their lives over the years.

Billy was touched by the memories. He both wanted and didn't want to hear more. How could he ever live up to the legacy Milt's husband had left? Why was he even thinking of living up to it when Milt hadn't given him even the smallest clue he wanted him to? He couldn't help himself from asking, "Do you think you'll ever love again?"

Milt rolled his eyes. "Really? You're asking me this?" He didn't seem angry or even offended by what Billy swiftly knew was an insensitive question.

Milt shrugged and then said something that caused Billy's heart to drop. "Nah. Once you've had a great

love like I did with Corky, how can you think of someone else? He's all I ever wanted." He smiled at Billy,
and there was something winsome and young in the
smile. It made Billy think of a little boy—and that image, he thought, was one that really made him fear he
was truly falling for this guy. "And he's all I ever will
want."

Billy nodded slowly. *I wish you hadn't said that. I
wish you'd given me just a little kernel of hope.* "Well,"
Billy said, sighing. "We should be getting back. See
what the damages are at your place, what you'll need
to get yourself fixed back up." At some point during
their conversation, Trixie had put their check on the
table. Myron's was the kind of place where you took
the check to the register as you were leaving. Billy
snatched it up. He shook his head when Milt reached
for his wallet. "Put that away. It's on me."

Milt frowned. "Come on! I owe you—for all
you've done for me. Let me pay." He leaned forward to
try to snatch the check out of Billy's hand.

Billy pulled back, grinning. "No way. My treat."
He winked. "You can pay next time."

Just as Billy stood, Milt reached out a hand to stop
him. "Sit down for a second. I want to say something
else."

Billy sat, expectant. "Yeah?"

"Yeah, I just wanted to thank you. For reaching out
to help when you didn't have to. But my gratitude goes
further than that. I also wanted to thank you for pulling
me out of my shell. Yes, I wanted to be alone, as I joked
earlier. I needed time to grieve, time to kind of try and
figure out who I was. Milt alone. I'd been Corky-and-
Milt for so long, I almost felt like I didn't have my own
identity anymore. So there was that. But after a time I

kind of *wanted* folks to talk to me, and they didn't. See, I think I'd cocooned myself for so long and so successfully, they sort of just gave up and left me to my own devices. Thought that's what I wanted, so I don't blame them. But I'd walk around the park with Ruby, and I started to feel like I wasn't even there."

Milt looked away for a second, and Billy bore witness to the pain on his features. He was quiet for a while, and Billy felt a stab of guilt for not trying harder to get to know this man, this neighbor whom he'd been lusting after since he first moved in. Mentally, Billy shrugged. He was like everyone else and assumed Milt was a loner, so why not give him his space.

Thank God for the storm!

"I really want to say thanks for making me feel visible, for making me *seen*. It's a greater gift than you know."

Billy thought briefly of how, when he was in the depths of his alcoholism and all the bad shit that went with it, people stopped seeing him because, he supposed, they couldn't bear to look at him—or worse, they were embarrassed to look at him. "Oh, I know. And I give you that gift freely, man, and with a great deal of pleasure."

"Okay," Milt said after a while, grinning, "breakfast is on me next time. And again, it'll be wherever you want to go."

"Okay. We'll go to Norma's next time." Billy smiled innocently, not mentioning that Norma's, in the Parker Meridian, had probably the most expensive breakfast in Palm Springs.

"Sounds good. Another Marilyn Monroe tribute joint?"

"Not really." Billy stood. He was glad they'd have another "date." And he'd have another chance, despite Milt's profession of undying love for Corky.

He had one thing over Corky, he thought, heading to the cash register with Milt behind him.

He was alive.

CHAPTER 7

MILT AWAKENED knowing something was different.

The house was dark and quiet. The old deco marble clock Corky had given him on their first anniversary made its soft whirring noise that Milt no longer noticed, save for in the quiet time of the early morning, when it seemed like the whole world was sleeping. He turned on his side, still missing Corky, even though they'd determined months ago that it was better that he sleep downstairs in the converted den so their night nurse, a guy named Ev, could keep a better eye on him.

The heat clicked on. This gentle blowing sound usually gave Milt a sense of security, and often, on nights like these, would send him back to sleep.

But not tonight. Tonight, for some reason, his senses were on high alert.

Milt reached out and touched Corky's old pillow, believing it still held traces of the Old Spice aftershave

Corky wore. It didn't, of course, but Milt liked to believe it did.

He sat up in bed suddenly, his heart throbbing.

Something was wrong. Something was off.

Although he had no logical reason to believe this, the notion was there, real and firmly implanted. He exhaled and swung his legs over the side of the bed. His slippers, parked there when he retired the night before, waited for him. He slid his feet into them.

He shivered. They turned the heat down to sixty-eight at night, and it felt even colder than that. Milt reached for his battered but loved plaid flannel robe at the foot of the bed and shrugged into it.

He crept down the wooden staircase, knowing each groan and creak by heart. When he got to the midway point, he shut his eyes and whispered, "Shit."

The door to the den stood open.

He and Ev always made sure to close it at night. Ev had recommended a lock on the door, because Corky *did* have a tendency to wander, especially at night, but Milt wouldn't hear of it. "I'm not locking him in like a prisoner," he'd told Ev.

Ev shrugged and quietly explained that it was for Corky's own protection. "It's not a punishment." Milt knew Ev, deep down, had zero hope of convincing Milt to see things his way, the sensible way, thus the soft tone and lack of conviction in his words.

Milt thought it was enough that Ev was there overnight. He stayed in the living room, which was right across from the den, so he could keep an eye on Corky.

Right?

Milt got to the bottom of the stairs and poked his head around the archway leading into the living room. Ev, in his jeans and blue surgical scrub top, snored softly on the couch, his head thrown back. On the TV, a braided and blonde little Patty McCormack was asking someone what they'd give her for a "basket of kisses."

Milt turned his head to peer in the other direction. Even though the den was dark, he could see the bedclothes on the floor, along with Corky's flannel pajamas.

"Oh no. Corky…." Milt sighed and went to the front door, which wasn't fully closed. Milt shut his eyes again and shook his head. *I'm never going to get a good night's sleep again, am I?* He called over his shoulder, "Ev! Wake up. He's gone again."

He listened as Ev grunted. The TV went off. In a second Ev, gray-bearded with a belly, was behind him, rubbing concerned brown eyes. "I swear, I just drifted off for a minute."

"A minute's all it takes," Milt snapped. He bit his tongue not to add, "What are we paying you for, anyway?" He flung the front door open wide and peered into the darkness. He turned back to Ev. "He's out there. Probably naked. Probably freezing. It's the fucking end of October, Ev."

The words made it all too real. Milt held back a sob, stuck in his throat.

"He's okay," Ev said, failing to hide how desperate he was. He stepped past Milt onto the front porch. Milt switched on the light, illuminating the wooden porch, with its swing and flower boxes, in golden light. The light spilled a bit onto the front lawn as well, and Milt could see the silvery frost that lay upon the grass.

He wanted to wail in despair. The yard, as far as his eyes could make out anyway, was empty. A cold breeze made him shiver and caused the branches in the maple near the porch to clack together, bereft of leaves.

"Where's my Corky?" he whispered, as much to himself as to Ev.

Milt stepped forward, hugging himself in a vain attempt to ward off the night's cold, and peered deeper into the gloom of their front yard. *Will this be the night it happens? Will we find him somewhere, curled up and no longer shivering? Will he have made that final transition?* Milt felt ashamed. In his darkest moments, when the caretaking had become almost more than he could bear and he was simply exhausted beyond any limit, he'd allowed himself to imagine what it would be like to be free of the shackles. It was for only a moment, a little fantasy, but Milt hated himself for even letting such a notion enter his conscious mind.

And now, with the horrible prospect facing him—a dark wish fulfillment—he hated himself even more. Wished he could banish that he'd thought, with relief, what life would be like without Corky for even a second. He whispered a fervent petition. "Please, please let him be okay."

Milt stepped down off the porch and onto the damp lawn. Below him, a few lights still shone in the valley in the little town of Summitville. It made Milt jealous, imagining the normal lives taking place just below him, even though he had no right to imagine anyone's life was less troubled than his own.

The blank and black space beyond the village, Milt knew, was the curve of the Ohio River.

Did he manage to get all the way down to the river? It was possible, even naked. The distance was only about a mile, all downhill. In his mind's eye, he could visualize Corky, muttering to himself as he made his descent down the cracked brick sidewalks leading to the river's edge. In Corky's mind he might be a boy again, off to do some fishing or to challenge the river's currents and swim out to the little tree-covered island in the middle.

Is he floating in the cold, cold water, caught up on some low-hanging branch south of town? Milt shivered, and this time it wasn't because of the cold.

In his reverie he hadn't noticed Ev moving behind him, but he did now.

"He's in the garage," Ev said, coming up to stand beside Milt.

Startled, Milt turned to him. "What?"

"He's just in the garage. Sitting on that old redwood bench. I threw a blanket over him. He didn't want to come with me, even though his teeth were chattering. I turned on the space heater you guys have out there too." Ev's dark eyes peered into Milt's own as though he were looking for an answer to the question "What do I do next?" which was most likely true.

Milt touched Ev's shoulder. "Thank you. Why don't you go on back inside? Finish *The Bad Seed*?" He chuckled, but there was little mirth in it. "I can take things from here."

Milt watched Ev as he headed back into the house. He felt guilty because he envied the guy a little. After all, for him there was an out from this nightmare. He'd finish his shift in the morning and could return to his normal life. As sweet, kind, and compassionate as Ev was, this was ultimately only a paycheck. When Corky passed one day, Ev would simply move on to the next person in need. Sure, he'd probably feel some sadness, some grief, but it would be nothing compared to the hole that would be left in the world for Milt.

Sighing, he turned toward the detached garage, his slippers sliding on the wet and partially frozen grass. The night air foretold winter.

The garage's single window glowed yellow. Milt entered through the side door, softly. He stood for a moment, regarding this man he'd pledged to spend his life with, for better or worse, and felt a sad smile creep across his own features. Corky was naked underneath the red-and-black Hudson Bay blanket Ev had wrapped him up in, yet he probably wasn't *that* cold. That blanket was a heavy mother!

"Bev! Bev... listen. And then we can go downtown with Gran, and she'll buy me a new Matchbox car at the five-and-dime. Yes, sir!"

Corky's smile lit up his features, making his dark brown eyes twinkle, adding more lines to his face, but somehow making him appear more boyish in spite of the wrinkles. He jabbered on to the person sitting across from him, his sister Beverly, taken from them years ago by breast cancer. Milt could almost see her sitting across from Corky, wearing one of the bedazzled sweaters she favored, her head shaved and her dark eyes looking bigger behind the oversized tortoiseshell glasses she always wore.

Milt then stared down at the oil-stained concrete floor, the tears welling up and threatening to spill over. *He's happy.* That much was plain to see. Corky had been tortured when his mind started going, when he couldn't remember things, when he'd been aware of the loss he was enduring.

But then things had changed as he fell farther and farther down into the well of his mind. The years erased themselves, and most of the time he lived as a boy again, innocent and happy. He truly didn't have a care in the world, most days.

Milt almost envied him. "Hey." Milt sat next to him and nudged him with his shoulder. Across from them, against the wall, stood the big box containing their Christmas tree. Would they take it out this year? Would Corky even be around to help trim it?

Corky looked over at him, a little surprised. Milt could see he was groping around in his head, trying to recall who Milt was. This would have hurt Milt once, but now it was just par for the course. He placed a hand on Corky's knee. "It's time for bed."

"Bed? Get out! I'm not tired." Corky's gaze penetrated Milt's. He looked a little surprised, maybe even a little annoyed, as though the hour was 4:00 p.m. instead of 4:00 a.m.

"Well, tired or not, it's very late. And we all need our rest." Milt thought about the long hours ahead of him, knowing that falling back asleep was nothing more than a pipe dream, the fantasy of a younger, untroubled man.

"I want pancakes," Corky insisted.

Milt sighed, and then he smiled. Corky had always told him that when he was a little boy and his mama would ask what he wanted for supper, his answer was always the same: "Pannycakes."

Milt shrugged. *Where's the harm? We're both up and awake now. What law says we have to lie sleepless in our beds for another couple of hours?* "You hungry?"

"Oh yes. I'm starving. I want a tall stack, with sausage *and* bacon." Corky licked his lips.

"That sounds really good. Coffee?"

"A gallon. Or, no, no, wait, how about hot chocolate? We have any of those little marshmallows?"

Milt nodded. The lump in his throat seemed to be growing in time with the knot in his gut. Yet he forced himself to say, "I can make all that happen." Milt stood. He knew it was no good to ask Corky why he was in the garage, why he'd shed his clothes and headed outside when the temperature hovered around the freezing mark. There were no answers, none that would make sense, anyway.

Milt started toward the door with Corky behind. Corky grabbed his hand, intertwining his fingers with Milt's. Milt paused for a moment, closing his eyes and savoring. He shut out the nagging, logic-based voice that told him Corky had no idea who he was. For all Milt knew, Corky could be grasping the hand of some old lover who'd been way before Milt's time. Or even his father or mother.

The point was, he was holding Milt's hand.

And that was enough.

In the kitchen he got Corky settled into one of the worn chairs around the maple table. This was after two quick stops—the bathroom and then Corky's room, to get him back into his pajamas.

Milt pulled the cast-iron griddle from the cupboard and set it on the stove to preheat. They'd used it so much there was no need for oil or butter. He could feel confident the pancakes wouldn't stick. He listened as Corky hummed "I Say a Little Prayer for You." The song seemed somehow an apt choice. It calmed Milt as he mixed together flour, eggs, milk, baking powder, and melted butter. He was too tired to make the bacon and sausage Corky had requested and knew that once he set a tall stack of pancakes before him, he'd forget about the protein part of the breakfast anyway.

Milt stopped stirring as Corky's humming morphed into singing. Corky had always had a beautiful and powerful baritone. It could break one's heart on a spiritual like "Amazing Grace." Now his voice, still lovely, was little more than a whisper as he sang the Aretha Franklin tune. The lines about staying in one's heart forever and that was how it must be just about caused Milt to have to leave the room.

He turned and looked at Corky, who seemed lost in the song, eyes closed. Milt wondered where he was… and if he could follow him there.

"You know I'll love you forever, right?"

Corky stopped singing, and Milt sucked in a breath, sudden. There was clarity for just a moment in those dark brown eyes. It was as though the old Corky had come back. He smiled.

"Yes, I know. Any other way would only mean heartbreak, huh?" He chuckled. "I'll always love you too. Two hearts, one love, like always."

Milt nodded, trying to swallow over the lump in his throat.

"Promise me I'm your one and only." Corky smiled, and damn it to hell, it *was* the old Corky. It was! "Forever…."

"And always," Milt said. He needed to turn away or he'd start blubbering. He went back to stirring the batter and realized the pancakes would be tough. He'd stirred too long.

But damn it, *he* was stirred.

By the time he turned back to Corky, he was gone. Not in a physical sense, but in a much worse way, really. His stare had returned to a kind of vacant glare. When he looked at Milt again, he seemed startled.

"What are you doing in my kitchen?" he asked.

Milt shook his head, trying with a tremendous force of will to give Corky his most reassuring smile so he wouldn't be afraid. "Makin' pancakes."

"Well, all right, then."

CHAPTER 8

BILLY PAUSED to take in the panorama.

He breathed in the mountain air, savoring the relentless sun, a golden orb directly above his head, beating down, warming, loosening his muscles.

Below, all of Palm Springs spread out, an urban desert sprawl. The airport, the green spaces, the clusters of homes, the golf courses, the commercial areas. Beyond, the desert displayed its barren ocher beauty, dotted here and there with pale green vegetation strong enough to survive the harsh sun and wind. The windmills, thousands of them, towered like bright white sentinels, some of their propeller blades turning. Billy had always deemed these turbines magical, something out of a science fiction story.

His gaze swept over what now was home. He was the king of the mountain.

Despite feeling like a king, though, Billy realized it would never happen.

Milt would never return the feelings Billy had been harboring for him ever since the very first moment he'd laid eyes on him, struggling alone to move in to his trailer.

Billy had tried. He really had. But every subtle hint he'd drop, every longing glance he'd send Milt's way, every awkward but pointed touch, Milt met by laughing off or turning away or, the very worst, with a glance that clearly said no.

And yet Milt really seemed to like him! There was a sense that they were becoming best friends.

Perhaps that was all they were destined to be. Billy could just about manage to live with that consolation prize, but in the dark hours of the night, when he'd stand outside in the desert heat with a moon casting its silvery glow over the trailer park, he'd wonder if maybe he wouldn't be happier gently but firmly cutting Milt out of his life. After all, sometimes it seemed like their growing friendship was, instead of a consolation, a hot point of pain, a tantalizing glimpse of what could never be.

Yet he couldn't bring himself to do it.

Milt made him smile.

Made his heart race.

Made—sometimes, when he was alone, eyes closed, muscles relaxed, fantasies firmly engaged—his dick hard.

Why oh why had this guy had such an effect? He was a good bit older. Really, he wasn't even all that remarkable-looking. Sure, he had a sexy kind of daddy thing going on, with his salt-and-pepper buzzed hair and close-cropped beard, his gray eyes that seemed to possess unfathomable depths, but honestly, if he were in one of the gay bars on Arenas, he'd look like almost every other man present.

Why couldn't Billy move on? Find a guy who wanted him, who was attracted to him, who wanted to be more than just buddies. The desert was full of likely and hopeful prospects.

Why was there this torture? This hope? Both things were doubly painful to Billy because he felt he had to endure them in secret.

It was almost enough to drive him to drink.

And sometimes he'd imagine dropping by Milt's with a fifth of vodka, something good like Stoli or Grey Goose, pouring strong and steady for both of them and watching the sun go down as their brains became fuzzier and fuzzier. Imagining a hand landing on a knee, a sorry/not sorry bump of shoulders, an impulsive kiss that just missed the recipient's mouth and then the aim would need to be rectified....

When those fantasies became too intense, Billy would find himself in need of an AA meeting, which he could almost always find, just down the road at Sunny Dunes.

Billy had to concede that Milt had come out of his shell a lot over the past few months. Billy could take some of the credit for that. He'd figuratively (though he wished it was literally) taken Milt by the hand and kind of forced him back into life. He introduced him around the little community at Summer Winds, letting him know whom he could trust and whom he might want to avoid.

He introduced him to Demuth Park and the pickleball courts there and taught him how to play. He got Milt out—to the Thursday-night street fair downtown, to the art museum, to a movie now and then. Milt's favorite theater was the Mary Pickford in Cathedral City—Billy smiled because Milt loved the big reclining seats—and Milt would usually be out cold within fifteen minutes of a movie starting.

But what they loved most to do together was hike the mountain trails, as they were this morning.

Now that it was October, the weather had turned decidedly more pleasant, almost cool in the morning, if you set off early enough. They'd usually do the Araby Trail or the one behind Vons supermarket, the trail Billy could never recall the name of. He'd heard many names for it, Clara something or other or the Goat Trails, but he just referred to it as the trail behind Von's. It seemed that's what most people called it.

He took a slug of water and watched Milt and Ruby now as they ascended farther up the Araby Trail. They were nearing the top, and the cluster of celebrity mountain homes, the most famous of which was Bob Hope's old domed mansion, was now below them. Billy rested against an outcropping of boulders, the sun beginning to actually burn on his shoulders. He was glad he'd smeared some sunscreen on his nose, donned a baseball cap.

When they'd started hiking in earnest, back at the end of September, Milt had discovered CamelBak water reservoirs on Amazon that he thought were a good idea. They were like mini backpacks that held a liter of water. He'd bought one for each of them, orange for him (his favorite color) and lime green for Billy.

Billy bit and sipped from the tube that connected to the pack's reservoir and felt a pang of deep gratitude. It was great to have an almost constant supply of water, while keeping one's hands free. It was also great to simply be surrounded by the ethereal beauty of the mountains rising up, San Jacinto just before them, crowned with rock outcroppings and topped with pines. Billy felt a spiritual connection with the mountains. There was a force, mysterious and powerful, that emanated from them, their thousands-of-years-old secrets encompassing the wisdom of the whole world.

Billy was grateful that the best things in life didn't cost a thing.

And he couldn't discount the beauty, the happy joy of the man and the dog clambering up the mountainside a couple hundred feet away.

Billy removed his baseball cap to wipe the sweat from his brow, to break up his matted-down hair, before putting the cap back on. He started up after Milt and Ruby, calling, "Wait up!" and laughing.

Ruby had turned out to be the most energetic of the three of them. She could race up and down mountain trails with all the agility and energy of a goat or a big-horn sheep. Milt stopped to watch her, and Billy came to stand beside him.

He was surprised when Milt laid an arm casually across his shoulders. The touch sent a tingle through Billy that sparked all the way down to his toes.

"She's come so far since I brought her home from the shelter when I first got here. Look at her go!" Milt laughed, and the sound was like music to Billy.

Milt's gaze focused on the dog, while Billy took in Milt's profile peripherally. Billy liked seeing the simple joy on Milt's face and the sun-reddened ridge across his nose and cheekbones.

"Did I ever tell you that, for nearly a week after I brought her home, she'd hide under the bed almost twenty-four seven? I had to coax her out with round steak and broiled chicken. Smart of me! I spoiled her right off the bat. Now she won't eat anything but.

"But God, she was a scared thing. I'd lift my hand to pet her and she'd cower, tail between her legs, terrified eyes looking at me, just begging. It broke my heart."

Billy watched the dog gallop around and thought that Milt could be describing another creature entirely. This girl was so sure of herself, so full of joy. He asked Milt, "Aren't you afraid she'll run away?"

"Ruby? Never. The sweetest thing about her is she knows which side her bread is buttered on. Whatever hell she came from, I firmly believe she knows it was me that rescued her from it. And she's grateful. She would *not* run away." Milt thought for a moment. "I'm grateful too—to have found her. She gives me as much as I like to think I give her."

Billy wanted to tell Milt that he was lucky to have such a faithful companion but knew he'd be pointing out the obvious.

Billy himself had been an abused animal, and the abuser had been the worst kind of enemy—himself.

He let Milt and Ruby continue wordlessly up the trail. Partly because not making the connection he wanted with Milt was making him a little sad, and with the sadness came a certain amount of lethargy. He'd hiked these trails—and this one in particular—countless times. They were aids to his recovery as much as the twelve steps themselves were, as much as the meetings were, and as much as his calls to his sponsor, an older woman named Candy. Alone up here on a trail, with the whole world spread out before him, he'd managed to find himself, to find the stillness within where he could begin to hear the voice that helped him find a new life, not hiding from it in a bottle, but embracing it, filled with all of its joys and sorrows.

Now he was lucky enough to have a companion on the trails. He'd taken Milt to White Water, to Palm Canyon, to Joshua Tree. There were still many, many unexplored paths for them. Could love grow in the sandy brush of the desert? Billy frowned. It didn't seem so, at least not in this case.

He sometimes thought Milt looked at him as a kid brother. There was an easy affection between them that was growing. Billy knew he should accept that, be grateful for the gift it was, but he was stubborn.

Today, he thought, shielding his eyes as he looked upward at Milt and his dog and a sky so blue it glowed with neon intensity, he'd need to beg off after their hike and get himself to a meeting.

He needed to remember the simple words of the Serenity Prayer.

CHAPTER 9

BILLY, BRAIN fuzzy, regarded the little crowd seated on folding chairs around him. The lower level of St. Augustine's Catholic Church looked like the basement of many other old Catholic churches, at least in Billy's experience. He'd grown up Catholic in Riverside, California, and had long ago abandoned the faith because, as a gay man, he no longer felt welcome. On the wall opposite was a come-on for Tuesday night bingo; next to that, Christ hanging out on his cross. Billy smirked. He'd always found Jesus kind of sexy, especially in that loincloth. There were also a few obvious nods to twelve-step groups—placards announcing "Easy Does It" and "There's a Magic in this Room" and "Just for Today."

What am I doing here? He shook his head, and the small motion made the little man behind his eyes pick up his ice pick and go back to work. The headache was sharp, making his eyes more sensitive to light. The fluorescents above, softly buzzing, did him no favors. He licked his lips, but it was no good—his mouth was dry. Acid pooled at the back of his throat.

The meeting hadn't started yet, and the men and women gathered in that basement room, with its speckled linoleum and acoustic-tile suspended ceiling, chatted softly among themselves, clutching Styrofoam cups of coffee, many of them laughing. Billy was surprised at that. After all, wasn't this an Alcoholics Anonymous meeting? Weren't folks supposed to be serious, or to underline with a groaner of a pun, *sober*? Some of these folks were behaving as though they were at a party. Billy felt left out, like he wasn't one of the cool kids. But how cool could you be, he wondered, if you ended up *here*?

The assembled alcoholics were a mix of young and old, fat and thin, poor (Billy guessed) and affluent. There were a couple of cute guys—one in particular who caught Billy's eye who reminded him of Freddie Mercury, with his cropped black hair and walrus mustache—and Billy wondered if he could lead him astray after the meeting. One woman looked like she could have no different occupation other than a librarian, with her gray hair pulled back in a loose bun and her oval wire-rim glasses. She wore a loose-fitting housedress, black-and-white checkered, that his mom would have referred to as a shift. She wore black flats—sensible shoes.

It must have rolled around to meeting start time, because a guy with a beer gut, reddish beard, and kind smile, seated in the center of the circle, cleared his throat. He smiled at everyone. "Would those who choose to please join me in the Serenity Prayer?"

Billy had heard of the Serenity Prayer but wasn't familiar with how it went. He'd be a good sport and at least try to mouth the words as they were spoken.

The man said simply, "God," and then paused.

There was a little shuffling of feet, a shifting of bodies; some bowed their heads.

And then they began speaking in unison.

"God grant me the serenity to accept the things I cannot change.

"The courage to change the things I can.

"And the wisdom to know the difference."

New age hooey, Billy thought. *What happens now?*

The bearded leader of the group began. "Hi, everyone, I'm Stan. And I'm an alcoholic."

"Hi, Stan!" everyone cried out in response, and Billy smirked, rolling his eyes.

Stan went on to describe how things would happen in the meeting. There'd be readings, followed by sharing and then "observance of the seventh tradition," and then announcements.

He might as well have been speaking in a foreign tongue as far as Billy was concerned. These folks had simply traded one addiction for another. He slouched in his chair, wishing he could be home, in his bed, sleeping yet another one off. He could get up later, find himself the greasiest cheeseburger and fries in town, and feel like himself again.

And then… a tavern near his apartment that opened early. Visions of a backlit bar danced before him, rows of bottles of different-colored potions reflected in a huge mirror mounted behind them.

He shook his head, trying to make himself listen, as Jon had told him, with an open mind.

But it was hard. And his ears didn't really perk up until the readings had gone by—so much gibberish—and a couple of people had shared their miseries.

But when the "librarian" began to speak, to share, Billy woke from his state of sloth and boredom.

Claire wasn't what he'd expected. What he'd expected was a woman who overdid the sherry after Sunday mass. *I mean, come on, her clothes make her appear like someone ready to bake cookies or maybe join some other old biddies playing pinochle at the senior center.*

"Hi, everybody." She smiled and met eyes with several of the people in the circle, Billy included. Billy was caught short by the warmth—and the inherent mischief—of that smile. Her dark brown eyes engaged with his for only a second, but Billy felt as though he'd been really seen.

"I'm an alcoholic named Claire." Her voice was raspier than Billy expected, a Brenda Vaccaro growl that spoke of too many cigarettes.

"Hi, Claire!"

Billy mumbled, "Claire," and gazed down at the floor, noticing some dried vomit on his shoe.

"Ah… what do I say? I'm grateful to be here. Grateful to be among you all, who help me on this sometimes twisted, sometimes tiresome road to recovery. We're all different, aren't we? And yet I see myself in each of your faces. I know your pain. I know your struggles." Claire drew in a deep breath.

Billy forced himself to look up.

"I know your joy too." There it was, that smile again—radiant and just a hint of "I've got a naughty secret." Billy began to wonder if there was more to this woman than met the eye. He had perhaps judged too quickly and too harshly.

"When I walked into these rooms, too many years ago for this gal to reveal, I was a mess. On the outside everyone thought I was on top of the world, a theater actor at the top of her game. I'd done major roles on the big stages in town—Steppenwolf, Goodman, Court. A little film work. Some TV. If you passed me on the street, I'd look vaguely familiar to you." She grinned.

Billy would have never assigned her the occupation of actor.

"But on the inside I was barely hanging on, honey. I'd leave the theater and head straight home. I wasn't big on drinking in bars. I had other uses for bars, which I'll get to in a minute. Ironically, the consumption of alcohol wasn't one of them. No, I'd go home, usually still floating three feet off the ground—that's what being on the stage did for me. I wonder why it wasn't enough? Anyway, I'd get home, and the first thing I'd do, after kicking off my shoes, was pour myself a shot of bourbon and crack open a can of Old Style."

She chuckled. "I was a classy broad.

"I'd tell myself the beer and the bourbon were just to bring me down after the adrenaline rush of being onstage. Amazing how many times I bought that line! But if it were true, I would have stopped after the first ones. Got myself to bed. After all, the booze, especially at first, brought me down quick, made me reasonably comfy, you know? But I kept going... and going. Like the Energizer Bunny.

"When I was drunk enough, that's when I'd go out. Hit one of the watering holes in my 'hood, which back then, was Lincoln Park. And I'd pick somebody up—anybody. I didn't care. Male, female, tall, short, fat, thin, rich, poor, black, white.... Just hated to sleep alone. Hated to *be* alone. Couldn't stand the sight of myself. To find someone who *saw* me, you know, and wanted me—that was the ticket. That was my addiction."

Claire paused for a long moment. Billy wondered if it was because she'd maybe crossed over into bitterness. Even from this short exposure to AA, he already knew the meetings were supposed to be about helping one another recover—not despair.

"What was my point? Hell if I know. Oh yeah, I wanted to talk about hitting bottom." Claire sighed, looking around the room as though she were gauging how she'd be accepted—or not.

"One night I met up with this guy, a kid really, couldn't have been more than twenty-two or so. Cute. Bit of a baby face. Sandy hair. Big brown eyes. The kind you don't know whether you want to mother or just fuck the shit out of. You know what I mean, ladies?"

A spasm of nervous laughter pulsed through the room.

"Anyhoo, we got to talkin', and he's all flattery and shit. Tells me what a nice figure I have, how I couldn't possibly be in my forties.

"I trusted him, you know. I was three sheets to the wind by the time he suggested we find someplace more private. Here's the thing about me and being loaded— most people couldn't tell. Whether it was genetic or years of faking being someone I wasn't, who's to say, but I could be shit-faced and you wouldn't have a clue. It's all about poise and diction.

"So we went out into the night. It was hot. You know how Chicago in August can be? Humid as hell, with heat that fairly shimmers up from the sidewalk." Claire left them for a minute. Billy could see it in her eyes. The place she traveled to wasn't a happy one. What she said next came out fast and low.

"Long story short. Keith, that was his name, tells me it would 'fun' to do it outside, since it's such a hot night. And I'm of a mind where anything goes. We traipse down to the lakefront. Remember when it was all big boulders at the end of Belmont? The gay guys used to hang out there.

"There weren't any gay guys there that night at the Belmont Rocks. There wasn't anybody. Too late. And I trusted my Keithy. He was a little boy. Harmless. Maybe even a virgin. It didn't occur to me that he would like the rough stuff." Claire let out a bark of bitter laughter. "Oh, but he did. He did." Claire nodded. She was silent so long, Billy wondered if she were going to speak again. So did several of the others, since they leaned forward, expectant.

"I won't catalog the abuse. Let's just say I can never hear someone say 'on the rocks' again without shuddering—for many reasons." There it was, that bitter laugh again. Billy wondered if Claire was beyond laughing joyfully. A pain rose up in his heart.

Claire shrugged. "He left me for dead. The three Bs, folks—bloody, bruised, and battered. Some kids found me around dawn at the bottom of the boulders. Broken ribs, split lip, both eyes black, face of a monster. Slacks around my ankles. Blouse eaten by the sharks." She hooted. "A couple more inches and I would have been in the lake and maybe no one would have found me.

"Yada, yada. An ambulance came. At St. Joe's, they patched me up, sent me to detox."

She smiled, and Billy was taken aback. It was radiant—he found the joy he'd sought earlier.

"And I am so fuckin' grateful to Keith and for that night because—ta-da!—here I am. And I might have never found all of you and a way to throw these fuckin' chains off if Keith hadn't taught me that painful lesson one August night so many moons ago."

There was a hush in the room, broken by Claire at last saying, "That's all I got."

People shifted their feet, looked around. Billy glanced up at the clock. The hour was almost up. Finally a few folks mumbled their thanks to Claire, and then everybody clapped.

Here's the thing. She looks like somebody's sweet old grandma. We never really know people from what we see on the outside, do we? I'll never judge someone again by the surface.

Silence. Billy was about ready to accept that they'd do whatever ablutions they did at the close of an AA meeting when Stan said, "We got time for one more share."

Like a classroom full of kids where no one has the answer to the teacher's questions, gazes darted away from Stan, down at the floor, at each other, wondering, "Will you be the one? Will you break the silence?"

Billy was stunned to find himself raising his hand. It was almost as though his arm and hand had developed a mind of their own. Everyone peered at him, and a rush of fire rose to his cheeks. He looked over at Jon, who nodded.

He tried to swallow but had no spit, so he just put some breath behind words and said them. "Hi. I'm Billy... and I'm an alcoholic."

"Hi, Billy!"

Shit. They say that to everybody. So why do I wanna cry? Billy choked down his sobs and his fears and just started talking. Those first words he'd just said were, really, the most important. Billy even thought for a second of that old cliché, the one about the journey of a thousand miles beginning with a single step.

Everyone saying "Hi, Billy" was standard, the voices tired, practiced, rote. But the moment wasn't standard. Not for him. It was an opening of arms. It was an explosion of release and relief. It was being seen, really seen, and not judged.

It was a moment Billy knew he'd never forget.

He grinned, knew it came out sheepish. His mind went blank, but damn it, he'd make himself speak even if he only uttered gibberish. He had to trust that the words would come.

The clock ticked down.

"I don't know what I wanna say. I *do* know what I wanna say. I just said it. I'm an alcoholic. A fucking alcoholic, just like my daddy and his daddy before him. Admitting that's more of a *thing* than I could have ever realized.

"I've denied it all my life, pretty much.

"I should have known when I took that first stolen beer with my cousins at age eight.

"I should have known when I was sneaking my parents' vodka before classes started in high school, watering it down so they wouldn't know. And finally, just pitching the bottle out when it was empty. What to do then? I was fourteen. How could I buy another bottle? Oh yeah, the answer came to me. Smile at the obviously gay guy coming out of the liquor store on Halsted. Maybe do a little more than smile."

Billy hung his head, then forced it back up, though he would look no one in the eye. Not yet....

"Replacing that bottle became a routine, one that started my signature move of mixing alcohol and sex. I was kind of a prostitute, huh? No, I *was* one. Booze instead of cash." Billy let out a long, shuddering sigh. He'd never told anyone any of this before.

"Gradually, I grew up. Didn't need to offer up myself for a bottle. I could buy my own. And I did.

But the pattern of drinking and sleeping with strangers continued. I even mixed it up with an alphabet soup of party drugs too. As I got older, I started hanging out in the clubs—there was T, G, X, all, of course, part of PNP." Billy shrugged. "It doesn't matter if you know what those letters mean—you get the gist. They all boil down to the same—running away from myself. Dulling the feelings. But here's the thing: I dulled everything, not just the bad shit, like low self-esteem and self-loathing, but the good stuff too, my compassion, my kindness, my simple joy.

"All of it went away. I drank myself through college at Loyola. Theater and voice major. Amazing that I managed to graduate.

"And I could sing! I didn't tell you that. I sang at open mics in coffeehouses and bars all over the north side. At one point, after I graduated and hooked up with a band, very briefly, I even had an agent interested.

"They said I sang a good song. They said I had a style." Billy smiled, wondering if anyone got the paraphrasing. He looked over at Claire and she winked, smiled back.

"It all went to shit. Even the singing. And yet it was the singing, the singing that led me here to you." He looked over at Jon. "You came to see me in my last gig, huh?"

Jon, arms folded across his chest, nodded. He didn't say anything, maybe because of the prohibition against cross talk Stan mentioned at the beginning of the meeting. Or maybe simply because silence really was one of the best ways of getting someone to talk.

Billy waved as though batting at a fly. Scratched the back of his neck. "I had the reverse Midas touch. Everything *I* touched turned to crap. That agent? I missed meeting up with him one too many times because I was loaded. That backup gig at Davenport's? Got fired my first night because I was too drunk to stand up." He laughed bitterly. "At least the show was over when that happened. Ah! I have a whole novel full of sad stories, all of them ending in tragedy.

"Poor me."

He glanced at the clock, wondered if the meeting should be ending at the top of the hour, thought he should wrap it up.

Somehow.

"But *not* poor me. Because I'm here. Because I'm Billy, and I'm an alcoholic. And I need help. Because my own will sure as shit hasn't done me any favors." He looked around the room, forcing himself to make eye contact with each person in that little circle. He thought he'd see those faces in his dreams, always. "And I'll be here tomorrow, or somewhere like this, and the next day and the next."

He hung his head low, staring down at the floor, and whispered, "Because I can't get better alone."

CHAPTER 10

MILT TOOK down two mugs from the kitchen cabinet.

He ground some beans, poured them into his french press, and then filled the electric kettle with water, plugged it in, and switched it on.

The radio, tuned to the local "nostalgia" station, MOD FM, on this December morning featured Peggy Lee singing "Fever." The song was seductive, almost bawdy, as it always was. Lee's smoky voice and the material were a perfect match. But this early in the morning, seductive and bawdy were a bit much, especially at high volume. Milt moved to the living area to turn down the stereo.

While he waited for the electric kettle to heat the water, he stood by the window to see what the day had in store for him. The sun rose in the east, and the colors were glorious, a blend of purple, gray, and orange. Ruby came to stand beside him, tail wagging, belly full of chicken, brown rice, and sweet potato—Milt's special blend. It was as though she too were observing the splendor of the morning sky.

He looked down at her for a moment and then back out at the just-after-dawn sky. "I made the right move in coming here, didn't I, girl?"

Ruby glanced up, warm chocolate eyes appraising. He almost expected her to nod, to agree. But other than a double thump of her tail on the floor, she kept her own counsel.

"I wasn't so sure when I got here last summer. The heat! Those triple-digit temperatures every single day. That storm!" The tile flooring in the trailer was new; so was the dark brown leather recliner. His other furniture had managed to emerge pretty much unscathed from the earlier flood.

In truth, the storm was a blessing because it had forced Milt to get rid of the olive-green scalloped shag carpeting that had been there when he bought the place. His old recliner had had to go too. It was way too similar to the one Frasier's dad had on the TV show of the same name. It was an old-man piece of furniture, battered, tatty, and on its last legs.

The new chair was stylish—it didn't even look like a recliner, but more like an elegant overstuffed chair. The flooring, flood-proof, the sales guy had assured him, was a porcelain tile that looked like distressed hickory but was much sturdier. The rising sun was just beginning to fall on it in slats now, which revealed to Milt that he needed to run the Swiffer around the place.

Winter was truly the season of heaven here in the desert. Clear blue skies and temperatures in the seventies during the sun-drenched days and going down to chilly lows of forties and fifties at night.

By the time he turned away from the window, Ruby had taken her place on the couch, curled up and snoring. The electric kettle made its little beep, letting him know he could mix up his morning brew.

He went into the kitchen, looked first at the french press, and then at the two mugs he'd taken down.

Two mugs.

He staggered back a couple of steps and plopped down on one of the stools he had at the kitchen bar. He covered his face with his hands and wept. Just like that, he went from serene, calm, and happy to sobbing so hard his eyes burned and his nose ran like a kid with a bad cold.

He allowed himself to wallow in sorrow for only a couple of minutes. Then he shook his head and stood. A roll of paper towels hung above the kitchen sink. He yanked one off and blew his nose, laughing at himself. "You're losing it, buddy."

He closed his eyes, giving himself just a moment or two more to calm and to get back to what passed for normal in these early morning hours. He poured hot water into the press, stirred it into the grounds, then set the plunger lid on top. Finally he set the microwave's timer for five minutes so the dark-roast beans could steep to perfection.

He moved to the counter and picked up one of the mugs—Corky's mug, he thought ruefully—and put it back in the cabinet.

When the coffee was ready, Milt poured himself a cup, added some of the french vanilla creamer he liked, and sat at the breakfast bar. "After all this time, man, after *all this time*. You're *still* thinking of him as being here." He took a sip and let out a sigh. "And the irony is he was *never* here. You came to Palm Springs to get away from the memories! To start over...." He laughed at the way he often found himself chatting away to himself these days. But hell, there was a lot he needed to work out. Still. And his rates as a therapist were, by far, the lowest in town, right?

Milt opened his Kindle Fire to check out social media and the daily news. He scanned the screen but couldn't concentrate. His mind kept drifting back to the two mugs on the counter, side by side. One was bright orange, Corky's favorite color, and it had a blocky, square handle. Corky had found it at the Goodwill store downtown and just had to have it. Orange was always his favorite color, favorite pop too. He'd found the mug in the store years ago, and its bright color had yet to fade, testimony to the pottery businesses in the area they'd lived in. Milt wondered how he could have set it out without thinking.

Milt turned his own mug in front of him, sending little ripples across the surface of his coffee. It was white, with the words "Palm Springs" in iconic midcentury modern lettering with a couple of bright yellow stars. He liked it because it held a lot of coffee and seemed to keep it warmer than other vessels.

Milt searched his brain for a dream he might have had upon waking. One where Corky might have had a featured role, thus explaining his absentminded yet significant error.

But Corky, sadly, hadn't appeared in a dream of Milt's in a very long time. At least not in one he could recall once the cobwebs of sleep were whisked away by his conscious mind. He'd dreamed of Corky a lot right after he transitioned and believed they were visitations.

He loved those dreams. He got to be with Corky again, and not Corky at the end but strong and sane Corky.

But now… it was as though his husband had moved on. Maybe he was up there in heaven, living it up and forgetting all about Milt down on earth, eking out an existence here in paradise.

Or at least what should have been paradise….

"Maybe it's time for *me* to move on," Milt whispered. In response, he shook his head. His lips formed the word no. He'd made a promise. Besides, he was too old to think of starting up a whole new relationship again. Too much bother. He had his dog, the neighbors, a good friend in Billy—and that was enough.

Why expose himself to vulnerability again? Why allow the potential for loss into his life? With Ruby and a simple life, he could be on his own and safe.

Right?

Thinking of Billy caused a pang of guilt to rise up in him. Milt knew the guy carried a torch for him, although he couldn't understand why. Milt had a good fifteen years on him, and the truth was, Billy was a hot guy.

He could do a lot better than Milt. At least in the looks department.

At least that's what Milt told himself when he'd catch Billy in a moon-eyed stare at him. Or when Billy would let his hand linger a little too long on Milt's leg at the movies together. Or when they'd kiss hello or goodbye and Billy made it obvious he'd like the buss to linger longer than one between friends.

But it seemed all Milt could see, in moments like those, was Corky's face, that sweet face, all innocent and full of trust and wonder. It would make any appreciation or ardor Milt felt for Billy fade like a rainbow after a summer storm.

He couldn't handle the guilt.

As though thoughts had the power to summon up a reality—and Milt sometimes believed they did—there was a small knock at the door, which caused Ruby to grumble and hop down from the couch. She padded over to the door, tail wagging, expectant.

Milt, echoing his dog, hopped down from his stool. The back door's frosted glass panel revealed little more than a human shape waiting out there.

Milt opened it, and a surprisingly chilly draft rushed in.

And Ruby rushed out. Her second-favorite human, Billy, was there, looking fetching in a sky-blue hoodie and jeans, holding a foil-covered casserole dish. Ruby danced circles around Billy, jumping on him and making soft *yips*.

"Ruby! Get off him." Milt laughed and opened the door wider. "C'mon in."

Billy edged by him, smelling clean—cold air and sage. He set the casserole down on the counter and squatted to scratch Ruby behind the ears.

He looked up at Milt and smiled. "I brought you breakfast."

Milt shut the door and moved over to the counter. "That's so sweet of you. I was just about to toast an english muffin."

Billy shook his head and stood. "This is much better. And better for you."

"Can I peek?" Milt didn't wait for an answer. He lifted an edge of foil and peered inside. Steam rose up. Yellow egg, dotted with green. The smell was amazing: peppers and onion, maybe even a whiff of some tangy cheese.

"It's my standard breakfast bake—beaten eggs with cheddar, green onions, and Anaheim peppers.

It's really tasty, if I may say so. It was so cold out this morning, almost freezing, which is rare in these parts, that I thought you might appreciate a hot breakfast."

"I do. I really do. Especially when you consider my standard fare is, well, toast."

They stood awkwardly for a few moments, grinning at each other. Rosemary Clooney, in the background, was telling someone to come on-a her house.

"So, you'll stay for breakfast, right?" Milt glanced over at the press to make sure there was enough coffee left for a guest.

"Considering I made it, I better say yes. Otherwise you might think I poisoned you."

Milt took down plates and pulled out silverware and set them up at the breakfast bar. He handed Billy a knife. "You want to cut?"

Once they were settled with big squares of what Billy called egg bake in front of them, Milt told Billy what he'd done that morning with the mugs.

"It's funny how stuff like that comes up and nips at you, out of the blue. And it's surprising how much it hurts." Milt took his first bite of the casserole. "Man, that's really good."

"Thanks. It's better with a little salsa on top. You got any?"

Milt shook his head. "I got ketchup."

Billy shuddered. "If you put ketchup on this, I'm out the door."

"Okay." Milt threw up his hands. "Mr. Gourmet."

"Milt, turning away an offer of ketchup in relation to eggs hardly makes me a gourmet. It makes me human with a few taste buds. Putting ketchup on this casserole would be like somebody in Chicago going to the Weiners Circle on Clark and asking for ketchup on a hot dog. Dude, in the Windy City, people get shot for less. Literally."

"No ketchup, then," Milt said softly, chewing.

They ate in silence, Ruby watching them, ever hopeful that something might accidentally-on-purpose drop to the floor.

"Coffee's good." Billy raised his mug.

"I can make another pot."

"I'm good. Too much and I'm jittery all day long. And I already had a cup at home." Billy finished his eggs. "So, you put out an extra mug this morning for Corky?"

"Yeah." Milt looked off into the distance. He kind of wished Billy hadn't brought the subject back up. He'd almost forgotten it, but like forgetting for a moment in a sleep-addled state that Corky was gone, his faux pas this morning cut deep. "You think you're over somebody."

"And then you roll over, expecting them to be next to you in bed," Billy said.

"Exactly."

Billy gave him a gentle smile. In light of what Milt knew of Billy's feelings toward him, he thought the smile was kind. "You know what you *could* do?"

"What?"

"You could allow yourself to, say, leave out a mug for Corky in the mornings. Or set a place at the table for him." Billy leaned a little closer. "What would be the harm?"

"That would be crazy. People'd glance in at me through the window and call the loony bin so they could send out men in white coats with butterfly nets."

"That's a lovely image. Not the men in white coats, but the part where I see you through the window, setting a table for two. That reminds me of a scene from *Rear Window*. You seen the movie?"

Milt nodded through a mouthful of eggs. "Love it. One of Hitchcock's best, in my humble opinion."

"You remember when Jimmy Stewart is spying on his neighbors and he sees a woman all gussied up? She's at her dining table, set for two, and she's talking away to someone, laughing, maybe even pouring some wine. And then you realize she's by herself. Did you think she was crazy?" Billy asked.

"No. I thought she was desperately lonely."

Billy said nothing. He finished his coffee. At last he walked over to Milt's picture window and stared outside. He became almost a silhouette in the bright sun, and Milt had a weird sense of déjà vu.

"I'm alone. But I'm not lonely." Milt began to gather up the dishes and then began rinsing them and then loading them into the dishwasher.

Billy turned. "Okay."

"You don't believe me." Milt felt a little punch inside. He perceived it as anger, irrational, but anger nonetheless.

"You're projecting, Milt. I never meant to imply that."

"Really?"

"Yes. I just thought it might be nice for you to re-member him in a simple way, like putting out his coffee mug in the morning. Instead of looking at it as an anti-dote to loneliness or insanity, you could choose to sim-ply see it as a gesture in his memory, a way of making yourself feel a little closer to him."

Milt thought of the orange mug in the cabinet. Could see it in his mind's eye. And he thought Billy, really, was awfully nice to make his suggestion. When he thought about it objectively, it wasn't so crazy or pathetic. It was actually kind of sweet.

Still, he didn't know if he actually wanted to implement doing something like that.

Silently, Milt finished loading the dishwasher, made the determination that it was full enough to justify running it, and then pressed the appropriate buttons to begin its cycle. He washed out, by hand, Billy's blue ceramic casserole dish, and then set it on a tea towel to dry.

He looked over at Billy. "What do you have on tap for today?"

Billy smiled. "Taking a little hike with you."

At the mention of the word "hike," Ruby's ears went up, more erect, and she hurried to sit by the door. She glanced back at Milt, expectant.

"Would you look at that? I think Ruby here has learned a new word."

"You up for it?"

Milt nodded. "It's been a while since we've been out."

ONCE THEY were a little way up on the Goat Trails, with the broad plain of the Coachella Valley spread out below them and Palm Springs proper bathed in golden light, Billy turned to Milt. "I've been putting off talking to you for a while. I have something I want to say."

Milt frowned. "That sounds ominous. Hang on." He pulled his hooded sweatshirt over his head and tied it around his waist. "I didn't expect it to be this hot." He looked at the flaming orb above them. "Old Sol makes all the difference...."

"Yep. Even though it's only in the low sixties. That sun just burns, doesn't it?"

They trudged onward and upward.

Milt asked, "You said you had something to say? I hope it's not bad news. You're not moving, are you?" He chuckled. "I've grown accustomed to your face."

"I'm not going anywhere." Billy sighed. "Let's take a break, okay?" He plopped down on a big boulder.

Milt whistled for Ruby to come back and she came running, tongue out, panting. She sat obediently at Billy's feet without even being asked.

Milt sat next to Billy and took a slug of water from his CamelBak. "You okay, buddy?"

"Sure I am. Wait. No, not really."

Milt cocked his head. "Your health's all right?"

"Yes, yes, although my liver is probably just biding its time." Billy chuckled. He drew in a big breath and let it out like a sigh. "Bringing you breakfast, asking you to come out on this hike on this gorgeous morning, were my ways of buttering you up."

"If you're looking for money, you're barking up the wrong tree. Once my bills are paid, I don't have any. I'm living off life insurance and the proceeds from the sale of my house in Ohio. Those aren't gonna last forever."

Billy punched Milt in the arm. "I'm not looking for a loan. Jesus." He paused for a moment—again—and Milt started to get worried.

"What is it, then?"

Billy simply blurted it out. "I want to ask you out. Like, on a date. We could do dinner or dinner *and* a movie. Not drinks, because, as you know, I'm a big old alkie, but food and entertainment and us, yeah. That sounds nice to me. Doesn't it sound nice to you?"

Milt stared off into the distance, drinking in the stark mountain scenery he'd yet to take for granted. Although he had to admit that, right now, he was a little distracted. "Billy," he started, gentle. "We've been through this." And they had, at least a handful of times. Milt didn't know if he could go on hurting the guy.

And yet a tiny voice spoke to him, inside. It seemed like this voice, whoever or whatever it was, was growing stronger and getting louder. *Why don't you just throw caution to the wind and say yes?* Milt racked his brain for the source, but he could remember someone, someone very wise, once telling him, "You don't grow with no." *Still, I can't. Much as I would love to spend more time with Billy. Sure, I'd love to feel his arms around me and vice versa. Sure, I'd love to kiss him, maybe even with our shirts, or more, off. I'd love to maybe even wake up one day next to him in bed.* This last thought brought Milt back to this morning and the mug. And how Billy had said something about waking and expecting someone to be in bed next to you. *Yeah, I get that. Corky was always there. How can I let someone else take his place?*

It would be cheating.

Milt was so lost in his own thoughts, his own turmoil, he barely noticed Billy speaking.

"I know, I know. And you told me how you promised Corky there could never be anyone else to take his place."

"That's right. I did. Near the end. So why? I can't go back on the promise I made to a dying man. Why do you want to put me in this position?"

Billy wiggled his eyebrows. "Because this isn't the *only* position I want to put you in." He laughed.

Milt chuckled too. "Stop it. I'm trying to be serious here." He felt a strange paradox within. Part of him wanted Billy to stop the flirting, the attempts to take their friendship to the next level. And part of him was deathly afraid that he would. Where would he be then?

You'd be right where you are now, Milt. Alone. Telling yourself you're happy with a dog, Judge Judy *in the afternoons, a frozen potpie for dinner, and turning in early because you're just so fucking bored with your life you might as well sleep it away.*

Milt knew it wasn't fair, to either of them really, to remain in this limbo.

Billy looked away from Milt but kept talking, low and slow. "Look, man, I like you. A lot. I have from the first moment I laid eyes on you." He held up a hand. "And don't try to argue. You've done that before, and frankly, you sound stupid. You're only a few years older than I am. You're a hot guy. I would be lucky to have you. You sell yourself short all the fucking time. I want you to know that you didn't just come to the desert to die and pine for your lost love. You want to pretend you're an old man, Milt, washed-up, when you're not. Not at all."

Billy sighed. "I know that sounds harsh. And maybe it is. But you need to hear it, bud. You need to hear it." He went quiet again, long enough for Milt to notice a plane taking flight off the runway of the Palm Springs airport far below. Long enough to wonder if Billy had said all he was going to say….

But he wasn't done.

"Look, man, I won't ask again, okay?"

Milt felt a chill run through him, despite the sun's intense rays.

"I need to move on if you're not interested."

Milt met Billy's gaze then, knowing he looked shocked.

"Yeah. Believe it or not, you've become so special to me, I've been postponing my life because of you, hoping you'd come to your senses and see what a catch you have right before you. Joke! I know I have more baggage than the lost and found at O'Hare." Billy shrugged. "But I know I have some good points. I try not to sell myself short.

"And hey, I don't want to be a cashier at Trader Joe's for the rest of my life. Not that there's anything wrong with that." He snickered. "But my name is Billy Blue. It's my real name! It belongs up in lights, on an iTunes playlist maybe, someone they gossip about in *People* magazine. Besides having a name, I can sing. I really can."

There was a long pause, yet the air hummed with tension, with expectancy.

Billy drew in a big breath. And when he let it out, he sang:

"Amazing grace, how sweet the sound
"That saved a wretch like me.
"I once was lost, but now I'm found.
"Was blind, but now I see."

Billy looked down at the sandy, pebbled dust at his feet, rubbing the toe of his left hiking boot in it. Milt was stunned to see the shine in his eyes. Tears?

Billy's singing voice was a rasp, but a velvet rasp that pierced the heart, penetrated both mind and soul. His was a gorgeous voice. Milt wanted to hear more, and he didn't. "Amazing Grace" was a surprising choice. Intuitive. Had he mentioned that Corky used to sing it at church? Corky's rendition was different, with his deep baritone, but just as stirring.

Hearing the same song, even just a piece of it, through two different instruments, voices, was eye-opening to Milt.

He found he could appreciate both. And there was no need to compare.

"You really can. Sing, I mean. Your voice is beautiful. Why that song, though?"

Billy looked up, smiled. "Ever since I've been in recovery, it's kind of been my song. See, Milt, when I was a drunk, I didn't think much of myself. I sure as shit had nothing or nobody to live for. Amazing grace is what we in the program call a higher power." Billy nodded, as though assuring himself of the truth of his words.

"For a long time, I've been coasting along on amazing grace, not quite lost but not quite found."

Billy peered into Milt's eyes, his blue-eyed gaze intense. "But now I see."

The gaze was too much for Milt. It hurt. He could see everything in it—Billy's attraction to him, his vulnerability, his simple need.

He wanted to give in. He wanted to be the grantor of a wish.

But.

But.

He didn't know.

It still felt like a betrayal.

And so he mustered up what he thought was all his will, all his courage. He mustered up his fierce loyalty for Corky, the man to whom he'd once pledged his heart forever—until death do them part.

And he put two fingers in his mouth and whistled for Ruby, who came bounding down the mountain. She'd learned well that high-pitched, piercing sound meant business.

"We're gonna go home now, okay?" It was hard for Milt to get the words out. His heart was clogged with disappointment and regret. Yet he felt he was doing the right thing.

Billy held out a hand, beseeching. "Just try, Milt. One dinner. Some gnocchi and marinara. I know a great place."

"Stop. Please." And Milt turned away because he couldn't bear to look at Billy. He started down the mountain, with Ruby leading the now-familiar way on the trail.

He didn't look back.

CHAPTER 11

WHEN HE got home, Milt threw Corky's orange mug in the trash.

He stared at it there for a moment, feeling a hot rush of shame, like he'd just committed a crime, murder maybe, and then decided he was being melodramatic. After a few minutes, he fished it back out and set it on the counter, like a too-bright accusation.

He started to feed Ruby her supper, then put her homemade food back in the fridge when he realized it was only a little after one thirty. Ruby didn't seem to care that it was too early and let out a frustrated *yip* of disappointment when she saw Milt putting the food back. She might have been saying "What the hell are you *doing*?"

He turned on the TV, watched for a full half hour, then shut it off when he realized he didn't even know what he was watching.

He tried to read a book (Stephen King's *Doctor Sleep*), gave up, and then tried a magazine (*Entertainment Weekly*), gave up on that, and attempted to surf the web.

He shut down his laptop after a few moments. Maybe if he went outside, into the brilliant sunshine and pleasant warmth, he could relax, feel like he wasn't running from himself. He remembered back home, as he still thought of it, and realized it was probably below freezing with snow on the ground and flakes of the stuff dancing in the air.

Ruby curled up at his feet, basking in the sun. Oh, to be a dog, with only the worries of where the next nap would take place and where the next meal would come from!

Milt prayed he'd come back in his next life in canine form, preferably looked after by a couple of doting gay men. That would be heaven, truly.

Milt considered heading over to the community pool for a swim, but even that seemed like too much effort, too much distraction.

Maybe he liked being miserable.

Maybe he liked torturing himself.

His rational mind told him that, in all honesty, Corky really wasn't a factor in his not wanting to simply go out on a date with Billy. Not anymore. Sure, he had promised, in a way, to be forever faithful. But logic told him that death wiped out such vows.

No one would blame him for seeking love, companionship, new happiness. The point was, he, Milt, was alive. And Billy was right—he wasn't *that* old. He shouldn't be pretending he was, acting as though his life were over.

He still had a lot of good years left here in paradise. Why shouldn't he, or why *couldn't* he, allow himself to make the most of them? Why did he think he needed to figuratively be forever dressed in black, with *widower* written in permanent marker across his forehead?

That's what he didn't understand.

Maybe he was simply afraid of getting involved again, of allowing himself to feel something, of letting his heart be vulnerable once more. There had simply been too much pain when Corky died. Hell, too much pain with watching him die—its long, slow progression. He'd been like a ghost, fading, fading away.

When he'd upturned his life and memories and moved out to California, he'd thought he was starting anew.

Now he wondered. Was he really beginning fresh? Or was he frozen in time? Had he changed only the geography but not the interior? His soul?

He closed his eyes. The warm sun felt good, relaxing, and it did what Milt wanted—provided deliverance.

CORKY SAT at the head of a long rough-hewn table. Gathered around it were a bunch of guys who looked Corky's age, as much as Milt could tell, because he couldn't make out their faces. They seemed to shift and flicker in dark shadows that surrounded them like a cloud.

Corky, however, shimmered in brilliant golden light.

He smiled as he played his cards.

Milt watched for a while, saw it was canasta. Corky's favorite game.

"C'mon, Gabe, it's your move," Corky said, seemingly in possession of his mental faculties.

Gabe, at the other end of the table, unfurled wings from his back and levitated off his seat.

Which struck Corky as so hilarious, he pounded a fist on the table, tears of mirth trickling from his eyes.

IT WAS dusky when Milt awoke. The featured colors this evening were purple, lavender, and orange.

Ruby's head lay on his thigh, and she stared up at him with pleading eyes. Love? Well, maybe a little of that, but the more plausible answer was hunger.

"Oh God, kid, you need your supper," Milt said, still groggy. Rubbing his eyes, he felt disoriented, as if he'd gained two hundred pounds during his nap, the slumber he never intended. It had taken him by surprise. He would have thought he was too keyed up to sleep.

He stretched, arms overhead, and looked around. There was a light on in Billy's little trailer, a pale yellow glow against the waning winter sky.

Milt wondered what he was doing. Whether he'd truly given up on him. If he'd blown his opportunity. A kind of longing coursed through him.

But it was longing he didn't have time to entertain, not with Ruby dashing back and forth between him and the back door, looking at him as though to say "Don't you get what I'm trying to tell you? I'm hungry!"

"Yes, yes, I know, little girl." Milt stood, feeling like the old man he thought he was. Lead flowed through his veins. His head was cloudy.

As he walked to the door, Ruby's tail-wagging increased proportionately.

"I'm coming. I'm coming," he told her.

He thought he'd had a dream, something about Corky, but he couldn't recall any images from it.

There was only a weird sense of peace—and Milt realized it was not for him, but for Corky.

AFTER HE'D eaten dinner—grilled rib eye and an arugula salad—Milt went to the window and peered outside, Ruby trailing close behind. He'd given her a steak too because he felt guilty about sleeping through her usual suppertime and for ignoring her. He was sure all was forgiven. She didn't let him out of her sight for a second, though, lest he should produce another steak.

The sky had morphed from its multicolored display into a deep navy with stars.

What are you looking for? Maybe you're checking up on Billy again, hmm? He shrugged, not wanting to admit the fact to himself. He forced himself away from the window. It only took a minute before he decided he needed just one more glance, just one more, and then he'd stop.

As he was about to pull away from the window a second time—because Billy's trailer was totally dark—Milt spied him, whizzing by Milt's own house on his bicycle. Milt watched his progress through the dark, staring after him until the reflector on the back of the bike disappeared into the dark, dark night.

Still restless, Milt sat down, picked up the remote, and aimed it at his TV. There was a rerun playing of an early *Roseanne*, when the show was still blue-collar and still good, and Milt watched for a few minutes the very realistic banter between the sister characters of Roseanne and Jackie, trying to engage with the show.

But it was useless.

His mind kept returning to Billy and their conversation on the mountain. *Just let it go. Let him go.* These thoughts repeated over and over, a litany, but they were like a few sandbags trying to hold back the rise of a flood in a storm. The thought of letting Billy go made Milt physically ill, and he wondered if his dramatic march off the mountain, along with his latest refusal of a date, had finally caused Billy to give up on him.

Milt couldn't blame him.

Milt wondered where Billy was headed on his bike. A jealous part of him entertained the notion that he was heading out for a hookup, someone he'd met up with on Craigslist or one of those sites Milt could never bring himself to explore, like Adam4Adam. Or maybe he was using one of those apps, like Grindr, that puzzled Milt even more. He'd met his Corky the old-fashioned way—in the back room of a leather bar. They'd had oral sex to completion before they'd even learned each other's names. Milt grinned at the memory. Perhaps things weren't so different in gay male cruising today; they'd advanced only technologically.

Yet Milt, imagining Billy off to some salacious assignation, wasn't as jealous as he would have expected.

And Milt realized that was because he didn't believe for a moment that was what Billy was doing. A vain part of himself opined that it was too soon for Billy. He couldn't possibly be hooking up, for heaven's sake. Despite any resolve on his part to maybe not see Milt again—to move on—Billy still had to be pining for Milt, right? Perhaps a song in his repertoire today would be "I Only Have Eyes for You."

Milt wanted to kick himself for the outlandish line of thought.

No, he really believed Billy wasn't meeting up with a man, because he suspected he was headed out to the Rimrock Shopping Center down the road. Every week there were dozens of twelve-step group meetings at a little unassuming building called Sunny Dunes near Von's supermarket.

Billy had told Milt he went there sometimes twice a day, for what he called "step study" or "round robin" and to meet with fellow recovering alcoholics. Milt wondered why he needed to go to *so many* meetings. Wasn't Billy cured by now? In one of their conversations while hiking, Billy had told Milt he hadn't taken a drink in years. Wasn't there a time when one was safely out of danger of relapse? Milt shrugged. He'd never understood addiction, not in any real sense. Maybe that was because he'd had so little exposure.

He wondered what meetings were like. And as he wondered, he was heading toward the bedroom to slip out of his sweats and into a clean T-shirt and jeans, maybe a hoodie. These days, temperatures plunged after the sun went down.

You shouldn't be doing this. It's an invasion of privacy.

Milt realized he didn't care. He was curious. And he attributed that curiosity to wanting to know Billy better.

He grabbed his wallet and car keys off the nightstand.

MILT SLID into the big room as quietly as he could. The meeting was already in progress and clearly very well attended. There were men and women of all ages, colors, shapes, and sizes sitting on folding chairs lining the walls. Some also sat in the center, at long buffet-style tables. Milt grabbed a seat near the door, doing a quick tally. There had to be at least fifty or sixty people in the room.

He'd had no idea there were so many afflicted people. And this was just one meeting in one night, in one city!

When Billy told him he attended AA meetings, Milt just assumed they were small, with just a handful of people in attendance.

But this was like a rally.

He crossed his legs as he listened to a redheaded woman with a fuchsia tank top and tattoos speak about her inability to stop relapsing. "I look at some of you guys, with so much clean time, and I want what you have, but I just can't figure out how to do it." She looked around the room, her gaze lighting briefly on Milt, which made heat rise to his cheeks. He wondered if she expected someone to offer guidance or perhaps a suggestion.

But everyone stayed silent.

She went on. "I guess someday it'll come to me. What I need to do." She shrugged. "For now, I guess I need to be satisfied with knowing that I'm willing—for God's grace to come to me, to show me the path. And I'll just keep coming to these meetings until something clicks." She smiled, and Milt could see a much younger, woman, prettier, in that smile—a glimpse of innocence and what might have been. "Thanks, everybody. That's all I got."

Everyone clapped.

There was a brief silence, and then Milt looked up as a familiar voice said, "Hi, I'm an alcoholic named Billy."

"Hi, Billy!" Milt found himself saying hi too.

Milt thought if he were a dog, his ears would have stood up at attention.

"I'm thinking about something I did once, back when I lived in Chicago. Someone gave me a butterfly kit as a gift. You guys know what that is? It's for kids, so that shows you how this giver saw me." He chuckled. "But it was actually really cool. A good experience. It let me raise a few butterflies from caterpillars on my own."

Billy paused, thinking. "I raised a few from caterpillar to cocoon to full-fledged butterflies, but toward the end, when I was down to my last one, I had a little trouble. This little guy just looked worn-out, sickly, couldn't lift his wings. I tried feeding him, poking him, prodding him, because, man, I have never been a patient guy.

"I thought he was gonna die. I remember it was a warm day, early spring, one of those days in Chicago when the temperature busts out into the sixties and you think you're gonna die from the sheer pleasure of it after the long and dark winter. So I took him out into the backyard of my apartment building, thinking if he was dying, he could at least do it in the sunshine." Billy smiled, and for a moment, Milt thought he'd spied him there in the back of the room, but then his gaze moved on.

"You're all probably wondering what this story has to do with anything. And I'm getting to that. See, for me, what I got out of this experience was the surprise I got when I took him out. See, he wasn't dying. It was just that his wings were very wet. When the sun warmed him up, it also dried his wings. In no time, I smiled as I watched him flutter off into the air."

Billy paused. Milt could see he was fully immersed in the memory. Milt felt like he was too; he could *see* that butterfly.

"My point, and I do have one, is that the little butterfly taught me something. Maybe not that day, but looking back I can see how I learned a little more about surrender, about just letting things happen on their own time, not mine.

"Like a lot of you, I'm a control freak. I want to influence the outcome of *everything*." He laughed. "Like right now. I know this guy and I really like him and I've been trying to get him to like me." Billy smiled.

Milt's skin prickled.

"And what I have to do is surrender. Things between us are gonna work out or they won't—and right now, it's looking like they won't. He's in a weird place and just not ready for the likes of me. Or anybody, really. But I know I just need to let go. As they say in these rooms, 'let go and let God,' and that's what I need to do. Surrender my will and just ask for my higher power's will to be revealed to me—whatever that is.

"One thing I know for sure, my higher power only wants me to have my highest and best good, right?" He nodded. "So I'm gonna try to surrender. Turn my will over. We'll see how that goes."

Milt caught the look of hope on Billy's face, like something shining and fragile.

Vulnerable.

And it cut to Milt's heart in an instant.

Milt stood and quietly slipped from the room as Billy's thanks and the subsequent applause sounded.

CHAPTER 12

IT WAS so hard to meditate. Even though Billy knew it was a good thing to do, it was almost impossible to quiet his "monkey mind." Yet he kept at it, making a time every morning to simply sit cross-legged on his bed. He'd set the timer on his phone for ten minutes, close his eyes, and try to relax and concentrate on nothing other than the slow in-and-out of his breathing. It seemed like such an easy task—just sit back and think of nothing. But Billy found it daunting.

He couldn't deny it. He thought he had one of the busiest minds on the west coast, maybe even in all the continental United States. The world? Billy shrugged and thought of an old Perez Prado and Rosemary Clooney song he loved, "Perhaps, Perhaps, Perhaps."

Billy had to chuckle. The song was appropriate for this morning. It was all about the pining of an unrequited lover for another—and about forcing him to make up his mind.

He sighed and basked for a moment in the clarity of the early morning sun. It was so delicious, he briefly considered simply flopping back on the bed and returning to sleep. At least in slumber, he could forget about his "problem" next door.

Yes, he'd seen Milt slip in and out of the AA meeting the night before. He was both thrilled and pissed off that he'd come. Thrilled because it showed, Billy thought, his interest in him. He was sure Milt wasn't coming to the meeting for himself. He'd known the man for a few months now, and there was no indication of any addictive behavior. Milt barely touched alcohol, save for the occasional beer on a hot day or a glass of wine with dinner.

Billy knew there was the chance Milt didn't drink around him out of respect for Billy's alcoholic status. That would make sense.

And he also knew, big-time, that alcoholics and addicts were masters of deception. Most all of them, Billy included, could lie and keep secrets with the best of them.

He just didn't get a sense—in his gut—that Milt was hiding something from him.

Ergo, he'd followed him to the meeting and listened to his story about the butterfly that referenced Milt himself. He'd snuck out right after Billy finished speaking, which lent validity to the notion that Milt had come expressly to see Billy.

It was heartwarming in a stalkerish sort of way, if that was possible.

He gave himself a break, grinning at what he'd just observed about himself—he had a very busy mind.

Stop it now. You need to meditate, calm that crazy head down.

You know what they say in meetings, in the books you read. Praying is asking God questions. Meditation is when you get your answers. But you have to be still. You have to allow yourself, and Spirit, the silence to answer, to move. You need to shut up and listen.

Billy took a deep breath, trying to absorb these thoughts deep within himself, not just as logical thinking, but heart thinking, emotive-in-your-gut truth-telling.

He set the timer on his phone and positioned himself so his back was against the headboard. He crossed his legs in a manner he called (despite it being politically incorrect) Indian-style, then opened his hands, placing them palms up on his lap.

He closed his eyes and drew in several very deep, slow breaths.

For a few moments, there was only the soft white noise of whatever machinery chugged inside his head. He could feel as much as hear his heart beat.

The thoughts came, though, much as he knew, on a conscious level, he was attempting to keep them at bay.

You can get through to him. You just need to do it in a way that's gentle, like approaching a wild animal that spooks easily. Just speak softly, hold out your hand, and let him know you have no agenda (even though you do).

"Quiet," Billy whispered. "Quiet." The word was his own little mantra. He spoke it, returned to his breathing, and tried to focus on an open mind.

And... thoughts like you just had are nothing more than you attempting to control the situation. Remember what you talked about last night at the meeting? The butterfly? Surrender? Not forcing things?

"Quiet," Billy whispered. "Quiet."

*Just let go. What will be, will be. Que sera, sera,
Doris.*

"Quiet," Billy whispered. "Quiet."

And Billy did manage to slip under for a few minutes, leaving his mind open and willing to receive.
Willingness was a big part of recovery for him, maybe
the biggest.

He leaned back and felt so at ease that, by the time
his phone's timer chimed, he'd almost fallen asleep.

He opened his eyes to a new world, sun-washed,
clouded only by a memory.

BILLY THOUGHT of all the jargon that was part
of "the program."

Referring to Alcoholics Anonymous as "the program" was just one such example. Others were: "one
day at a time," "easy does it," "keep coming back," "let
go and let God," "expect miracles," and "we are only
as sick as our secrets." There were many more, built up
over the years with one purpose in mind—to keep the
alcoholic or addict in a state of active recovery, rather
than a state of active disease.

The one Billy was thinking about as he slid back
into the world from the relaxed state his meditation
induced was an acronym. SLIP. It stood for "sobriety
loses its priority" and referred to fucking up. You drank
again. You used again. You let sobriety take a back seat
to other concerns.

Some people in the program regarded any falling
off the wagon as a relapse. Others called it a "slip,"
hence the acronym. A slip didn't seem as bad as a relapse. A relapse seemed more full-blown—more epic
in terms of failure. A relapse was going on a drinking
binge that lasted for weeks, months, even years. A slip

was having a beer at the company softball game. Not so bad, right? A little white lie.

But Billy's first sponsor, his guardian angel, Jon, who took him to his very first AA meeting, had told him there were no degrees of severity when it came to relapse. Jon used another phrase they were fond of in meetings, "one is too many and a thousand is never enough."

Drinking again, whether a little or a lot, was a fail. No matter how much or how little one had, drinking again put you right back into the active disease of alcoholism.

Billy had slipped, relapsed, let sobriety lose its priority, only once. And for that he *was* grateful. In his years of going to meetings, he'd seen way too many "chronic relapsers" and knew how much easier a slip could become once you allowed yourself one, then two, then three, until it seemed you were back on the merry-go-round that was anything but merry.

Yet for some reason, this sunny morning, the memory of his fall, that singular fail, was with him, strong and stinging, like a shot of Patron agave tequila.

The ironic thing was, he'd gotten his one-year chip only the week before. He recalled the meeting where Nick, the "chip monk," had awarded Billy the little round plastic memento of sobriety. There had been tears of joy on Billy's part and applause and cake for the rest of the assembled. They'd sung "Happy Birthday" to him, off-key, but no song had ever sounded more beautiful.

Everyone was happy for him because they all knew what it took for him to get there.

Billy had walked out from that meeting on a pink cloud, feeling he was safe. He would never touch a drink

again. He was *cured*. He simply didn't want a drink—
ever. He could picture beer mugs, shot glasses, cham-
pagne flutes, and more in his head, and they were nothing more than permutations of that semisolid known as
glass. The liquid in them? Ah, he could take it or leave
it. He chose to leave it, and it was no skin off his nose.

He drank again four days later.

The funny thing about that slip, Billy thought, was
that it ambushed him, taking him by surprise.

A slip like his could be compared to a slip outside—on an icy sidewalk on a winter's day. One moment you were tooling along, minding your own business and sure of your footing. The future seemed clear
and certain. The next moment—*boom*—you were on
your ass.

This one happened suddenly, with no more of a
trigger than boredom. Saturday night and Billy had a
gig. A gig at a small divey-type bar in Wicker Park. A
gig that got cancelled because it was so frickin' hot in
Chicago that night that the bar's AC went out and they
shut down, knowing no one would want to sit around in
the insufferable heat. All over the city that night were
brownouts and blackouts.

Billy sat around for a while in his un-air-condi-
tioned studio in Rogers Park, in only his boxers, with
a big fan blowing more hot air on him. His body was
slick with sweat. He sipped a sweaty glass of sweet tea.

And he was horny.

And he couldn't sleep, even after a double-header
movie marathon on TMC—*Imitation of Life* followed
by *Written on the Wind*.

It was eleven o'clock, the temperature outside was
still ninety, the humidity index almost the same, and
not one leaf stirred on the big maple outside his front

window. The air stunk of Lake Michigan, car exhaust, and roasted corn from the Mexican vendor cart down the street.

Billy paced the little room he called home, feeling pent-up, bored. The image of a tall glass of beer, with a head of foam just sliding over the edge and beads of condensation up and down its sides, tortured him. Had tortured him for a while. It had come into his head, unbidden, about halfway through *Written on the Wind*.

And it stayed there, even though Billy knew that by giving this TV-ad image headspace, he was conjuring it into being. Life worked that way.

He knew he should shut the TV off, dim the lights, position the fan toward the foldout bed, and crawl into it to lie naked upon the sheets, praying that by morning the air being sucked in by the fan would feel at least tepid. Praying that he would wake with dawn's diffuse light still clean and sober....

He knew he should call his sponsor, Jon. Early on in the program, when Billy was faced with temptation, all he needed to do was to pick up the phone and call him. God bless him, Jon never failed to answer his phone, and if need be, he'd come over to Billy's place within a few minutes. After all, they lived in the same building. Talking to Jon, or even some of the other people on his phone list, always forced away the urges. It was as though by naming the urges, he was shaming them—the desires skittered away into their dark corners.

But that cunning little demon inside wouldn't let him pick up the phone. Why? Because Billy knew it would work. He'd call and Jon would talk him down. He'd ask him if he really wanted to throw away a whole year of sobriety. He'd remind him of how much he'd given over the past twelve months to work the steps and to build a new life for himself.

Billy knew these things already. And he didn't want to hear them.

For to hear them would mean he'd eradicate the need. He'd go to bed. He'd be safe for another day.

And he didn't want that.

He shut down his thoughts as he took a quick shower and dressed in a pair of camouflage cargo shorts and a wifebeater tank top. He slid into a pair of flip-flops. Taking stock of himself in the medicine cabinet mirror, he decided to run a handful of gel through his hair, giving himself what he thought of as a very fetching golden bedhead. He even winked at himself.

He laughed.

He didn't question. He didn't ponder. Most importantly, he didn't slow down.

He grabbed his keys off the desk by the door and headed out into the languid night. No breeze stirred the air or the leaves on the trees. The air felt almost like glue, like he was wading through it. Thick.

His car, a beat-up Ford Pinto wagon, was over on Jarvis. It had wood paneling on the sides and was a dusky shade of harvest gold.

It was ancient. But it still ran.

As he slid into the driver's seat, he allowed himself one thought. He'd be at Touché, the leather bar at Clark and Devon, within a few minutes.

And damn it, he could have that beer.

TOUCHÉ WAS crowded. Hot, sweat-slicked men pressed against one another, elbowing for room at the bar. In the back room, a full-scale orgy took place in the big room's darkest corners. A boy who couldn't have been more than legal age sat on the pool table, legs splayed apart, shorts around his ankles, as various men took turns sucking his porno-movie-sized cock while he calmly drank a Bud Light, almost as though he wasn't aware of what was going on farther south on his anatomy.

Billy wondered if the boy was high as well.

The boy was a temptation, but not as great a one as what awaited him at the bar. As Billy approached the less-crowded bar here in the back room, he was almost trembling with need. His gut churned. He was sweating even more than the heat dictated. His eyes did a tunnel-vision sort of thing, closing in on the bear bartender in his faded Levi's 501s, combat boots, and studded leather harness setting 'em up with a smile. He had a thick dark brown beard, hairy chest, and gorgeous dark chocolate eyes. But Billy was more interested in the taps he was effortlessly working, from which foamy magic gold poured.

Billy was grateful that things weren't as close in the back room. He could make his heart's desire come true that much quicker. He could barely wait for that hoppy first swallow.

He got up to the bar at last, got the bear's attention, and smiled.

"Hey, handsome, what can I get you?"

Billy almost blurted out "beer" as they did on movies and TV, but he knew he had to be more specific. What the hell? While he was being more specific, he might as well add in a little something to jump-start the party.

In for a penny, in for a pound.... The old adage had been Billy's excuse for abuse for years.

"Gimme a shot of Jack and a Bud back."

The bear winked. "You want that Bud on tap or in a bottle?"

"Bottle."

Billy looked around the bar at all the other horny, wicked men getting loaded, the rises and falls of their conversations the husky music of desire and seduction. Anita Ward was imploring someone to ring her bell over the speakers. Somewhere near the back, a glass shattered on the floor, followed by laughter and applause.

And then—the shot and the beer were in front of him. Hungrily, guided only by need and instinct, Billy reached for them.

The bear smiled. "Slow on down there, stud. You want me to run a tab for you? Or you want to pay as you go?"

Billy laughed, feeling a little sheepish. His credit and lack of funds had long ago precluded his owner-ship of a credit card, so a tab was out. He groped in his pockets, and his hand curled around a crumpled bill. It was a twenty.

He had a moment of clarity and thought of all the booze that bill could buy. Not a ton, but enough to at least get a pleasant little buzz going.

But another thought came to him, one of rational-ization and control. "Keep the change," he said.

The bear picked it up, eyeing him—and then the bill—with a lopsided grin. "You sure?"

Billy wasn't sure at all. He nodded. *This way I won't overdo it.*

He downed the shot. After not having drunk for a year, it was like a line of liquid fire going down his throat. He choked a little, and the bartender chuckled.

Billy cooled the flame with a long swallow of beer. It tasted like something the gods had made, yeasty, cold, and delicious, tamping down the heat from the bourbon.

The bartender must have been amused, thinking Billy was a novice. He also might be attracted, but Billy was never sure about bartenders. He could never tell if they were angling for a tip or truly interested.

In any event, he poured him another shot of Jack. And another after that.

"I find that if you get a couple down, the ones that follow go down smoother and smoother."

Billy licked the whiskey from his lips and gave the bartender what he thought of as his most winning smile. "I'm Billy." He stuck his hand out over the bar.

"Joe." The bartender shook his hand, wiggling his forefinger into Billy's palm while never taking his gaze from Billy's eyes. "Why don't you pull up a stool? I've got some other guys to take care of, but it won't take me long. Maybe we can get acquainted?"

Okay. So it's safe to assume he's into me. And if I smile pretty, flirt a little, I might not have to pay for another drink tonight. Let him think we'll go home together once the lights come up. Billy planted his ass on one of the black vinyl stools.

He had no intention of going anywhere with Joe after the bar closed. But he'd take all the free drinks he could charm his way into.

And it barely crossed his mind that what he was doing was little more than prostitution.

Billy chatted with Joe for the next couple of hours—about the heat wave, the best pizza in town (Pequod's in Morton Grove), Madonna, and the scandals taking place a few feet from the bar. During all this talk, Billy, growing increasingly soused, managed to keep up the currency he needed in exchange for the booze

Joe freely poured—a lopsided grin here, a raised eyebrow there, a wink or a few seconds' worth of meaningful eye contact.

Old Joe, Billy thought, through the haze of his growing buzz, thought he'd be getting a little somethin' somethin' tonight. He almost felt sorry for the guy.

Billy worked him like a musical instrument, and the song he was playing was Toby Keith's "Get Drunk and Be Somebody."

By the fifth beer and the seventh shot, Billy was certain Joe had fallen in love with him and was planning china patterns. He too was more than a little tipsy (after all, he'd matched Billy pretty much shot for shot) and was finding it hard to tear himself away from Billy's charms, despite being implored, often forcefully, by outraged customers sick of being ignored.

Billy had to admit he felt their outrage was justified. But what could he do, other than raise a glass to their irritation?

By the time Joe shouted out, "Last call! You don't have to go home, but you can't stay here," Billy was plotting his escape. Even drunk, he felt shame about how he'd manipulated and used Joe, but he comforted himself with the fact that it probably wasn't the first time Joe had fallen for such crap. Billy told himself the guy should know better.

Joe rapped his knuckles on the bar, and when Billy looked up at him, grinned. "You want to come by my place? Smoke some weed? I just live over by Touhy Park."

Billy actually considered it—for all of a few seconds. For one, he was so drunk he thought he could only be a disappointment to Joe. He'd either fall asleep or throw up, maybe both, and hopefully not in that order.

Joe didn't need to see that. No, Billy convinced himself, he was actually doing the guy a favor by ditching him.

Billy stood on unsteady newborn-colt legs and said, "Gotta take a whiz."

"Come right back. Okay?" Joe called after him, the hope in his voice heartbreaking. Almost.

Billy did stop in the men's room. Fortunately, it had cleared out and the bright lights revealed cigarette butts, toilet paper, a crumpled phone number, and a used condom on the concrete floor. Ah, gay love! So tender, so beautiful.

Billy pissed, proud that all his copious stream went into the urinal and not on his flip-flop-clad feet.

He staggered out into the front part of the bar. Only a handful of guys milled around, hoping, Billy guessed, that slim pickings would lead to their reward. Billy experienced a moment of pathos for these guys, so lonely, really, and hoping to quell that need for company by taking home a stranger. He figured the same scenario was being repeated right now at bars all over the city. Hell, all over the world.

How many of these one-night stands would end up as a meaningful connection? Billy shrugged. The pessimist in him thought not many, but the realist told him that odds were a few guys just might find their Prince Charming, right there in a bar stinking of sweat and beer.

He'd forgotten all about Joe as he headed out into the still-hot night. A guy on the corner, waiting, Billy guessed, for a southbound bus, smiled and gave him the eye. He was cute, couldn't have been more than twenty-two or twenty-three, with a platinum buzz cut, blue eyes, and clad in denim cutoffs and a red tank.

Kid, you're barkin' up the wrong tree.
Now where did I park?

THE FATIGUE really hit him as he drove north on Ashland Avenue. The euphoria he'd felt up and left, like an inconsiderate trick who dresses and creeps out while you're asleep.

At this wee small hour of the morning, the thoroughfare was pretty much deserted but still blighted with stop signs at almost every fucking corner.

Suddenly the giddy high brought on by the whiskey and beer had morphed into despair and exhaustion. Billy just wanted to get home, where he could collapse into bed and sleep, perhaps forever. He could visualize the mussed-up pullout sofa bed, his Holy Grail. So what if it smelled like sweat? It was his personal heaven.

He just needed to attain heaven—and fast.

Fortunately, there was a shortcut. Since there was no one around, he didn't really need to observe all these damn stop signs, plus the occasional roundabouts that went with them. There was nobody out on the road anyway, so what was the harm? Blow right on through 'em!

As he rolled through yet another intersection, his bleary-eyed gaze revealed another car approaching on the opposite side, headed south. *Good night, brother. Make it home safely.* He gave a little salute toward the headlights as they slowed and passed him.

When he looked in the rearview mirror, though, he saw the car hang a U-turn.

"Shit," he whispered, when he realized it was one of Chicago's finest.

The blue-and-white cop car didn't put on its siren, only its whirling blue lights, but started after Billy. He could almost hear the *Jaws* theme music in his head.

"Fuck," Billy whispered. *I can get away. I know these streets like the back of my hand.* He made a quick right and headed east for a couple of blocks, then rushed down an alley going south, ignoring potholes, then swerved left to head west on Sherwin Avenue. He did all of this at a speed topping out at close to eighty miles per hour.

He thought he'd lost the cop by the time he pulled up behind his building. There was a parking lot back there with only a few spaces, spaces that required paying rent to use them. But sometimes the renters didn't come home and the spots were left vacant for the night. Billy saw one of those spots and accepted its emptiness as an invitation.

He allowed himself a little sigh of relief, followed by a shaky snort of nervous laughter.

As Billy pulled into the one open space, thinking he'd rouse himself early and go out and move his car before the towing service the locals referred to as the Lincoln Park Pirates spirited his Pinto away, not one cop car but three pulled in behind, blocking him in. All had their blue lights whirling, along with spotlights, blinding, trained on the Pinto.

"Well, that didn't last long." Billy threw the car into Park and then snatched the keys out of the steering column.

Sweat poured down from his hairline and trickled, crawly, down his spine. His heart did the Watusi. He pounded the steering wheel three times, each time saying the word "Fuck."

He no longer felt drunk. Quite the opposite, in fact—he felt amped, clear-headed. The fight-or-flee mode engaged, despite knowing that neither was an option.

Billy sighed and got out of the car.

The headlights, all facing him, made him squint. *What am I supposed to do now? Raise my hands? Get down on all fours?* Billy, being mindful to walk in a very straight line, moved to the back of the Pinto. He simply stood there, squinting.

The lights were so bright, he couldn't really see any of the cops getting out of the cars, though he could hear doors slamming. He wondered for a moment if Jon was looking down from his window at the scene. Wondered if he'd be available to bail him out one more time.

They circled him, black silhouettes against the lights. Somehow, through all his drunken days and nights and ill-advised times behind the wheel, he'd never had a DUI.

He figured his luck was up tonight. *So be it. I shouldn't have taken that first drink. Why did I throw it all away?* He shook his head, wondering how the sobriety he'd been so mindful of, so careful about building, had tumbled down, fragile as a house of cards, in the space of only a few hours. *How could I be so stupid?*

Finally one of the police officers approached. She was close enough that he could get a glimpse of her face—a pleasant one, if not a very happy one. She had dark curly hair, and in a better light, he was pretty sure he'd see blue eyes. South Side Irish, maybe? She was a little hefty, and when she got up next to him, she didn't wrinkle her nose or anything but raised her eyebrows in a way that reminded him of a mother used to dealing with mischievous children.

"In a hurry? Got someplace you need to be?"

The jig was up. There was no reason to create some story to try to bargain his way out of this mess.

One thing he'd learned from the program was that you were honest, and when you saw where you did wrong, you promptly corrected it. In fact, that was pretty much the tenth step.

Billy had yet to work all the steps, but he knew them by heart. They repeated them at every meeting.

He blew out a sigh. "Nah. Just wanted to get to bed. I am so tired."

The officer nodded. Her smile had morphed into a little smirk, and he wondered what was next. Walk a straight line? Touch his finger to his nose? Breathalyzer? Whatever the test, Billy knew his goose was cooked—all of them would have only one result, drunk as a skunk.

People sometimes brought court cards to the meetings so the group secretary could sign and validate that someone was doing his court-ordered recovery work.

Billy thought he might soon be one of those folks. What a shame. Worse, though, would be the shame of walking into the next meeting and raising his hand when the leader asked if anyone had less than thirty days. Did they want a welcome chip and a hug? Billy thought of the year chip he had in his pocket, earned so very recently.

Damn.

He didn't even think it would be worth it to ask the officer to cut him a break. He'd been driving drunk, bad enough. But he'd also evaded arrest, leading Chicago's finest on a merry chase. He'd be lucky to get out of this with only a DUI.

Voices squawked from the walkie-talkie strapped to her shoulder. She nodded to his building. "You live here?"

Billy nodded eagerly. "Yes, ma'am. I guess I was just a little too eager to get home and hit the hay."

"And you're done for the night?"

"Oh yeah, for more than the night, actually."

He chuckled. She didn't.

"Hang on." She left him to consult with the other officers, who'd stood around, arms crossed.

She returned in a minute. She was smiling. "Okay. I'm going to let you off with a warning." She pointed to the wooden stairs at the back of the building. "You just get your butt inside. And in the future, please watch your speed and your observance of traffic signs." She looked at him, and her eyes said so much more than her lips. They were saying something like *Buddy, you escaped a world of trouble tonight. By the skin of your drunk-ass teeth.* "Okay?"

"You got it, Officer. And thank you so much."

"As I said, watch yourself. Don't be afraid to call a cab."

And she walked away. Billy watched them all get back in their cars and, one by one, speed away. He surmised something had probably come up on those squawking walkie-talkie voices, something more important than his transgression tonight.

Either that or he really did have a guardian angel. Who got out of hot water like this with only a warning? *Dude, don't even ask. Just be grateful.*

He had to sit down on the bottom step outside his building because he was trembling so violently. For a minute he thought he was going to puke, even tasted the hot acidic bile at the back of his throat, but he was able to keep it down.

After a while he got up and went inside.

NOW BILLY remembered the slip and was glad to know he'd never taken another drink since that night.

Now he could enjoy this brilliant morning sun as it was meant to be enjoyed, without wincing at its brilliance or feeling nauseous and wanting to pull a blanket over his head. Now he had an appetite for breakfast when he got up. Hair of the dog was just that, the literal stuff that Ruby shed when she and Milt stopped by. He no longer got the shakes.

Best of all, the urge to drink had all but disappeared.

Everyone deserved a second chance, even a third or a forth. And if we want something bad enough, and if it's good and right, we don't give up.

We believe in it. We set our intentions. We don't make it happen, but we do let *it.*

Billy looked outside just in time to see Milt and Ruby emerge into the morning.

He smiled.

He'd open the door to possibility. But first, he needed to make himself some breakfast.

CHAPTER 13

MILT HADN'T seen Billy in what seemed like a long time. In reality it was most likely only a week—or less.

But length of time really didn't matter. Not where it counted—his heart. He was certain he'd closed the door on the possibility of having any kind of relationship with Billy, including a friendship. It made him sad, but there was a part of him that told him it was for the best. He knew that pushing Billy away was his own doing, yet he still couldn't help pining for his smile, his nearness.

It was the age-old battle between head and heart. And Milt was exhausted with trying to figure out who might emerge victorious.

Sometimes it was easier to simply live, to exist.

He took his dinner out of the microwave—a Marie Callender's chicken potpie—and set it on the stove to cool a bit. Ruby, alert to the smell of chicken, jumped down from her perch on the couch and padded out to the kitchen, claws clicking on the linoleum.

"Ah, you know what's good, girl. Don't you? Don't you worry. You'll get some." Milt rolled his eyes and squatted down to rub her behind the ears in a way he knew she was particularly fond of.

When he was done, he washed his hands. Then he set out a bowl for his pie. He liked to overturn it and then break it all up with a fork. It wasn't complete until he'd ground lots of black pepper over it and added just a shake or two of Parmesan cheese. These potpies were a guilty pleasure and probably the chief cause of his recent weight gain.

What did a few extra pounds matter when the only ones who saw him naked these days were poor Ruby and the man in the mirror? He might as well follow up supper with a big glass of milk and a couple of those terrible but delicious store-bought boxed chocolate doughnuts he'd picked up on his last trip to Ralph's. On that trip he'd also treated himself to Cheetos, Cherry Garcia ice cream, and a box of frozen corn dogs.

Feeding your loneliness? he admonished, knowing it was true.

He'd thought about texting Billy a couple of times and had even gone so far as to pick up his phone and begin tapping the tiny keyboard. The days had been beautiful for hiking, and Milt had wanted company.

Yet he could never bring himself to do it. He wasn't sure why. Oh, he had his ideas—irrational ones about cheating on Corky or not being ready for a new man—but those ideas didn't hold water. Not really. For one, they were just getting tired, like a comedian with the same old shtick.

Whether it was Billy or not, one day Milt would need to get out and meet some people. Make some friends, at least, of the two-legged variety. He knew Palm Springs was rife with gay men of a certain age, and there were meet-ups and social groups for interests of just about every stripe. There was volunteer work. Hell, he could even break down and get himself a job. Starbucks was always hiring, right?

Back in Ohio he'd always been the sociable one, urging Corky out of the house to go up to Pittsburgh and see a Broadway touring production, or arranging to have people over for dinner or to play Cards Against Humanity. Milt was always the one to suggest taking a class, joining a club, even simply hanging out at the Elks club in downtown Summitville.

He'd enjoyed people.

When had he lost that?

These days Milt often began mornings with plans for checking out a museum (the art museum was free on Thursdays), a website for a Coachella Valley performance venue, a new hiking trail beyond the ones within walking distance of the trailer park (there were many; Joshua Tree, for example, had dozens of hikes), even the Yelp reviews of the gay bars along Arenas Road.

Mornings often held the promise of a new life.

But then he'd retire to bed far too early, with none of the goals met. Ruby didn't mind as she curled up in the crook of his legs.

The theme music for yet another episode of *The Golden Girls* lulled them to sleep almost every night. The pathos of this was not lost on Milt.

He sighed as he sat down at the breakfast bar to make a mess of his chicken potpie and to devour it.

Talk about pathetic.

He aimed the remote near his bowl at the TV. Amazon Prime had a series of video dramas based on the works of Philip K. Dick that he'd been meaning to check out. "No time like the present," he said to Ruby, who appeared to be listening with eager ears. But even Milt knew she couldn't care less what he was talking about. She was looking forward, he knew, to the supreme ecstasy of licking the bowl clean when Milt was done. He called her cleaning dishes this way the dishwasher's prewash cycle.

Just as he was navigating to Prime Video through his Roku, there was a knock at the door. Milt smiled and shut the TV off.

It didn't matter who it was. It was company. Even if it was just one of the neighbors with a piece of misdelivered mail, it would be another human being to talk to. An encounter with a real live human being…. *Wow.*

But when he opened the door, Milt was genuinely pleased and, oddly, confused and conflicted.

Billy stood just outside his kitchen door.

And God, Milt now knew for sure the definition of the adage *a sight for sore eyes*. Even though he was only clad in a pair of jogging pants and a Superman T-shirt with his feet bare, he looked breathtakingly sexy. Wasn't that always the way, though? Men who worked the least at it were often the most alluring. He eyed Billy, maybe even undressing him a bit with his eyes, and came to the conclusion hardly any man on earth could possibly look better.

Without warning, experiencing such unexpected joy, Milt blurted out, "I love you!" It took him more by surprise than it did Billy, who took a step back and cocked his head.

Billy laughed. "What did you say?"

"I, uh, I said—" Milt swallowed, his mouth and throat suddenly very dry. "I said I'd love for you to come in."

"Oh. Okay." Billy brushed by him.

Ruby, of course, went nuts, panting and leaping up on Billy, almost bowling him over. Milt sometimes jealously thought she preferred Billy to her very own master. His dismay at this thought was tempered with the notion that he couldn't blame her.

Billy *was* kind of fun to be around.

Milt chuckled as Billy got down to wrestle with the dog, who was acting as though she never got any attention or exercise. It seemed she'd completely forgotten the chicken potpie. She had her priorities straight. Men over food.

Milt would do well to listen to his dog, at least in this moment.

When they were through, Billy stood up and surprised Milt with a bear hug. And it wasn't just a quick nice-to-see-you-again hug, but a deep, lingering squeeze that could easily qualify as a cuddle.

When Billy pulled away, Milt was disappointed, feeling almost as though Billy took a part of him with him as he retreated. "What was that for? You nearly took my breath away."

"Because I'm glad to see you. Aren't you glad to see me?"

Milt looked toward the TV and its blank screen, as though an answer to Billy's question might be broadcast there. But the black screen mocked him, offering up no words of wisdom or even a distraction.

"Of course I am," Milt said softly. *I'm gladder to see you than I should be.*

"Okay, then." Billy glanced at the kitchen counter where the "deconstructed" potpie steamed. He pointed. "Supper?"

"It's a Marie Callender potpie." Milt scratched his chin as heat rose to his cheeks. Corky used to tease him about his love for junk foods. "Anything processed feels like Mom's home cooking to you," he used to say.

And he was right. Milt had grown up in the heyday of convenience food. His mom had delighted in TV dinners, Tang instead of orange juice, Hostess fruit pies, and TV Time popcorn. The truth was short-cut chemical-laden foods made him nostalgic. He suspected the same was true for a lot of folks growing up during his era. For Milt, they were the equivalent of Mom's apple pie.

"I see your disapproval," Milt said. He slid the bowl down the counter toward Billy. "Take a bite."

Billy grimaced and then laughed. "I've had them before. They're, um, good." He took a step back while, at the same time, Ruby took a couple of steps forward, her nose in the air, twitching.

"See? Ruby knows."

"Look. I didn't come by here to eat potpie."

"Oh? I thought you did." Milt grinned.

"No. I came by because I wanted to talk to you, but since I see you're just about to sit down to eat, I'll come back in a little bit." Billy moved toward the back door.

"Okay," Milt said, knowing he should forego the pie for now. *Be present for your guest.* Billy was his gift on a lonely weeknight.

The pie would reheat just as easily in the microwave.

There'd been a strain between them. Billy, he thought, might be here to fix things, to remove the awkwardness that had sprung up between them. Wouldn't that be nice? Wouldn't that be wonderful?

From out of nowhere, a little voice in Milt's head told him, *Maybe things are better left as they are—broken....*

And at that thought, the strangest thing happened.

Milt felt a sharp rap to the back of his head. He whirled around, frowning, to look. Of course, there was no one behind him. He gingerly touched his head. He knew his face must have gone quizzical and confused because Billy peered at him strangely, a question in those blue eyes.

"What's the matter? You okay?" Billy asked.

"Weird."

"What's weird?"

"I could have sworn—" He waved away the rest of the sentence. Saying it out loud would just be, well, too weird. He suspected Billy thought he was odd enough without his adding to the impression.

And then he got a chill. Because one of the things that annoyed him most about his sainted husband, Corky, who could do no wrong now that he was gone, was that he would always give Milt a quick rap to the back of the head, playful, when he thought Milt was out of line. It was never abusive and only in good fun, but there were times when Milt got so irritated by it that he came close to hauling off and punching Corky—seriously. Hard. Corky never should have done that. Yet he did. Repeatedly.

In casting Corky only in the golden light of memory, he'd obliterated most of his less endearing qualities. With each passing day without him, Milt made Corky more and more perfect in his mind until the man approached sainthood.

Now that the sensation had vanished, Milt questioned whether he'd actually felt it at all. *Is my mind just playing tricks?*

Or is something more going on here?

Billy put his hand on the doorknob, poised to open it. "I'll come back. Eat your supper."

In his reverie, Milt had almost forgotten he was there.

"Don't go," he blurted out. More than anything, he suddenly didn't want Billy to leave. He sensed something vulnerable and precious in this moment and feared that if Billy left now, they could never recapture it.

Billy's face, up until that moment a bit confused, relaxed. He smiled. "You sure? It's no problem. You might have forgotten I live just behind you."

"Don't be silly. The potpie will reheat." Milt had an idea. "Or I can heat one up for you. I've got more in the freezer. Chicken, turkey, beef—even a chili-filled one. I haven't tried that variety yet, so no promises."

Billy grimaced. "That's okay. I already ate."

"Liar." Milt chuckled. "But please stay and let's talk."

An uncomfortable silence, lasting a full minute or two, followed.

Billy finally broke it by moving into the living room. He plopped down on the couch. "Okay," he said on an exhalation. He stretched his long legs out before him.

Is there anything more beautiful than a man's bare feet? Milt was surprised at the thought, having never had any particular fondness for that portion of a man's anatomy, yet Billy's feet suddenly made Milt feel he could almost write an ode to them.

Milt hovered by the breakfast bar, not wanting to give in to the irrational yet colorful urge to go all

Mary Magdalene on Billy and get down on his knees and wash those sexy bare feet for him. He had to put a quick hand to his mouth to contain the laughter, aching to burst out. *You, Milt Grabaur, are a crazy person.*

"Are you gonna come in and sit down or what?" Billy asked. "You can eat that mess, excuse me, your dinner, while we talk."

Suitably shamed, Milt picked up the bowl with the potpie and set it on the floor. Ruby leaped on it, and Milt thought he'd be sorry later. It took her all of one minute, maybe even slightly less, to get that whole potpie in her tummy.

"You didn't even taste it." Shaking his head, Milt sat in his recliner, across from Billy.

"So." Billy eyed him.

"So," Milt said, sitting too straight, muscles tensed.

"I feel bad about how things have been between us ever since you came to the meeting at Sunny Dunes." Billy looked away, down at the floor, as he said, "But I felt a little like you invaded my privacy. If you wanted to come to one of my meetings, to see what they're all about, you should have asked me. I would have taken you."

Milt nodded. Part of him wanted to be defensive and ask, "Aren't the meetings open to the public?" But he knew Billy was right. He'd been sneaky and deceptive. He should have at least asked how Billy might feel about his being there, especially since he was there for no other reason than to see Billy, even if it was to somehow know him better.

"I'm sorry, Billy. I don't know why I followed you that night." Now it was Milt's turn to look down at the floor, abashed. "Well, that's not true. I do know."

"Why?"

"Because I wanted to know you better, to see what this important part of your life was all about." Milt looked at him, trying to ensure his smile was gentle. "I just want to know all sides of you—not just the whole parts, but the broken ones too. Lord knows, we all have them." Had he revealed too much? "I'm sorry if you feel I invaded your privacy. But I'm *not* sorry I went to the meeting. Your story, about the butterfly? It was beautiful. I don't think I'll ever forget it."

Billy shrugged. "It's just my truth. I have to work hard on surrender. I have to take it to heart and remind myself that doing so isn't about being weak. It's about being strong. Becoming powerless can, paradoxically, make one power*ful*."

"I got that."

"It's about not controlling." Billy sighed, threw his hands in the air for a moment. "Yet here I am tonight, about to try to control something." He laughed. "We are so imperfect. Us human beings. Don't you find that to be so, Milt?"

"Oh yeah." Milt regarded Billy and thought this moment felt good. They were two men acknowledging *not* their weakness, as some might say, but their vulnerability, their humanity. "I want—" Milt began but couldn't finish. What *did* he want, anyway? To be relieved of being a perpetual widower? To be delivered from his horrible fear it would make him somehow less than human? That it would make him selfish to desire new life and, even, just maybe, new love? Did he want to be made callous?

"What do you want, Milt?"

The words came without warning, without conscious thought. The words that came were unexpected, yet when Milt uttered them, they rang as true as anything he'd ever said in his life. "To be seen. Isn't that all anyone wants?"

Billy's hand leaped up to touch his heart. He looked at Milt then, really looked at him. It was as though he not only peered at him but peered *into* him. "I see you," he said softly.

"I know you do. And that's what scares me."

"Why would that scare you?" Billy leaned forward and then sat back again. He patted the couch next to him. "Come sit beside me, okay?"

Milt wanted to. And yet he wasn't sure he could— for to be that close would make him vulnerable, would open a door to something he couldn't be sure he was ready for. He leaned back into the recliner, so hard it almost made the footstool extend. "I don't think I will, Billy." As soon as the words were out of his mouth, Milt ached to take them back.

But he couldn't. Not yet.

Again, a sharp rap to the back of his head. "What the hell?" Milt shouted, rubbing at the now-tender spot on his scalp.

Billy laughed, and the odd tension in the room broke just a little. "You are nuts."

"I am. Totally. I think I went off the deep end the day I realized Corky wasn't coming back." Milt sucked in a breath. Again, he hadn't expected to say what he did. He wasn't sure what he was going to say but knew it should have been something more mundane, something more pedestrian. He'd never been much for revealing his innermost feelings. He said, in a hushed tone that he wasn't sure was even audible, "I broke a long time ago. But I couldn't let it show. Someone needed to be strong." Milt bowed his head. "It had to be me. I wasn't given a choice. And if I had been, I would have chosen to take care of Corky, even as he got more and more impossible. To the very end—when he no longer recognized me." Milt's voice caught, and the lump in his throat grew. He stared down at the floor for a long time.

And then he got up and moved to sit on the couch beside Billy. Billy leaned over and hugged him, pulling him close. "Is this okay?" he whispered in Milt's ear. Milt thought it was nice of him to ask. Billy recognized and *saw* his boundaries and respected them.

In response Milt simply reached up to put his hand on the arm that was around him, to squeeze it. He nodded.

They stayed like that for a while, maybe even longer than Milt realized. It was long enough for Ruby to come into the room, circle around several times on her fleece bed, and then lie down. Long enough for the hurt Milt felt during those final days, taking care of someone with dementia, being all loveless and selfless, to dissipate. If he were being perfectly honest, there were times back then when he'd wanted to say the hell with it all and hide away in bed, the covers over his head. He'd felt so much guilt about those feelings and now, right now, with Billy close, he realized he needed to forgive himself. He'd done the best he could.

The people who loved him back home called him a hero. His best friend, Dane Bernard, had pleaded with him to put Corky in a home. "The one out in Glenmoor is very nice—they'll take good care of him there. You can be with him every day, still. But they'll be around for him at night so you can get some rest. They'll make sure he doesn't get into trouble, wander off, harm himself."

Dane's advice had been heartfelt. He'd only been looking out for Milt. He'd wanted only what would be best for him—and for Corky. Milt knew, even back then, the constant caregiving and vigilance had worn on him. He could see it when he looked in the mirror—and a prematurely gray and weathered older man looked back at him.

But he couldn't do it—at least, not until the very end, when it was only a few days until Corky would, mercifully, draw his last breath. The thing that stopped Milt from doing it sooner was always the same. He had only to think of Corky and his occasional moments of clarity "coming to" in some sterile nursing home room and wondering where he was. Milt could clearly picture the look of hurt and confusion on Corky's face, and he'd known there was no way he wouldn't be in this fight until the very end.

And he was, even though there were a few days in the nursing home. He'd done the good thing. The selfless thing. The thing everyone praised him for, telling him he was a saint and that there was a special place in heaven waiting for him. They'd mostly said this at Corky's wake, adding that he and Corky could one day be together again.

Finally, Milt wriggled just a bit to politely break the hug. He scooted over, away from Billy, so he could talk.

"I just realized something," Milt said. "I'm still doing it. I'm still caring for Corky. I'm still here for him." Milt smiled sadly and looked toward Billy to see if he understood what he was saying. It *was* a little crazy, wasn't it? Still caring for a man who was beyond care? Still caring for someone who was buried almost a year ago?

But then Billy, God bless his empathic and caring soul, put some perspective on things. "You're not crazy. You're just grieving, Milt. That's normal. I'm being selfish, wanting something from you that you're not ready to give. It hasn't been that long. In a way I'm jealous of you for having what you did with Corky— and for so long. I've never really had that, and sometimes it feels... hollow."

Milt wanted to ask, "How do you know what I feel?" but thought, quite sensibly, that now was not the time to argue but to listen. In some ways Milt realized he was more than ready to accept what Billy had to give. *Just look at those feet! Imagine what they're attached to.* And for a moment Milt pictured working his way upward from those feet. On his knees. Until he arrived at that beautiful, radiant, and caring face. *Stop! We're talking about Corky here.* Milt let that thought sink in, and then he thought *And that's just the problem.*

Milt wondered what to say, caught as he was between his loyalty to a man he'd loved with all his heart and soul, a man with whom he expected to spend the rest of his life, and the desire to free himself from the very shackles his heart imposed. His head told him it wasn't terrible, or even unhealthy, to want to reach out for a new person, a new life, to move forward, upward, any direction away from the wallowing and the pain.

But because it was his head talking to him, Milt was mistrustful. He knew his heart told him the truth a lot more often.

But what to say to Billy?

Fortunately for Milt, Billy again had the right words.

"Earlier I said I was here trying to control things, and I just realized I'm not. I know I'm powerless over your grief, and I suspect you are too, for now. So I'm here for you. Not to control, not to push my own agenda, even though I know, in the end, it'll be you that benefits most from that agenda." Billy gave him a wink and a smile. "Joke. I'm here because I wanted to say that I'll take whatever it is you want to give me. I don't want to pressure you.

"Here's what I propose. That we start seeing each other again. By seeing each other, Milt, I mean only hanging out. Hiking. Seeing a movie. Having breakfast at Myron's Café. Me cooking you something decent for dinner." Again, that smile.

"Not dating. Lord, no! Just hanging out."

Milt felt two things arise at once inside him—disappointment and hope. Why wasn't life simpler? Black and white? Milt chuckled in his mind as he thought *Black and white like Corky and me?* Again, he wasn't sure what to say. The old heart-head conundrum was really confounding him tonight. If he went along with what Billy was saying, it felt like settling, like admitting defeat. If he challenged it, he knew the lover of Corky would rise up once more, chastising him for being untrue to his memory.

He wondered if he could ever win. *Will I be trapped in this limbo forever?*

"Would you be willing—for us to see each other again?"

Milt nodded.

"Good. And I'll say this—when, or if, you want to change from calling it 'hanging out' to dating, we can do that." Billy grinned. "Okay?"

Milt nodded again. *My, aren't I eloquent tonight?*

"Good." Billy stood. "Now I'm gonna leave you alone. Partly because I don't want to break the spell here. And partly because I want you to have just a little more time by yourself to grieve, to think. I know you need it. And I'll give you that space."

Billy moved toward the door. With his hand on the knob, he said, "Two weeks. I'll come over in the morning two weeks from now to pick you up. We'll take a hike. Okay?"

"How do we know the weather will be okay for that?"

"Dude, we're in Palm Springs. The sky's always blue."

"You got a point." Milt grinned. "Okay."

"Two weeks. Bright and early."

Milt watched Billy leave.

What had he done to deserve such kindness? And unbidden in his head, Corky's voice rose up, the one before he was taken ill, and it said, "You really have to ask?"

CHAPTER 14

It took forever for two weeks to pass.

Billy kept himself busy, trying not to notice the snaillike passage of time. He went to meetings, of course. He shared. He set up the coffee table. He stacked chairs after. He led one meeting. He did the closing prayer at another.

He worked at Trader Joe's as usual and even put in for extra shifts, stocking shelves, unloading trucks, or filling in as a cashier when someone couldn't make his or her regular shift. Extra money was the bonus; the real reward was the filling of time productively.

He meditated. Maybe he did it more than ever during this self-imposed two-week period, where he was trying to show Milt how selfless his feelings were. He also wanted to demonstrate in a very real way his powerlessness over other people. He'd sit on his bed with the morning sun warming his back and let his body relax and his mind go blank, using his favorite mantra, the word "quiet." During those times, he'd trained himself enough to actually still (well, almost) his monkey mind enough to get some answers, to know he was on the right path with Milt and, more importantly, himself. Sometimes an image would come to him of the two of them together, Milt's head on his chest as they rested on sun-drenched sheets. Sweet.

He read. Right now he was going through the "big book" of Alcoholics Anonymous. He'd read it more times than he could remember. But like the Bible for some people, each journey through its stories and guidance he'd discover something new to give him hope, to ensure his progress. Within those dog-eared and well-worn pages, there was a connection to his fellow alcoholics and, more importantly, to his higher power, whom Billy saw not as some judgmental figure in the sky, but as a radiant being within his own self, shining and whole, representing his highest and best self. The words on those pages lifted him up and let him know that, no matter what, he wasn't alone.

His first sponsor, Jon, back in Chicago, had given him the "big book" as a gift at Billy's second meeting. Then its cover was glossy and its pages pristine. Now it looked old, tattered, its spine in danger of breaking, but Billy could never dream of giving this particular copy up. It had taken on the power of a talisman over the years. He knew he'd miss not only the highlighting and the notes in the margins. He'd long for those coffee stains and the small tears. Most of all, he'd miss the quiet energy the book had given him—as if it embodied Jon McGregor himself, that kind and caring angel who, once upon a time, had saved Billy's life.

And when he wasn't meditating, reading, working, or going to yet another meeting, he was dreaming. See, even though he was respected and liked as a Trader Joe's cashier, he still thought about singing, about sharing his voice. He didn't think it was vain to say that it was a gift. To say that, for him, was only expressing gratitude. Billy wanted to simply *give* so much, not for himself or for fame and fortune, but so he could touch another's heart with his voice, with certain lyrics he adored because they were so universal and true.

Singing for him was never a performance. It was never about attention or adulation. It was a collaboration with whatever audience was before him. He broadcast his voice, his message, and if the magic worked, his listeners then took it into their hearts and made it something meaningful—in their own lives.

Oh, how he missed that. It had been a long time since he'd actually sung in public. He was hard-pressed to recall the last time.

He thought if things didn't work out with Milt, he just might take himself away from Palm Springs. He could be packed up and ready to move within a day. His trailer was only a rental. There was an excitement in thinking he could simply hit the road and head over to LA, or back to Chicago, or even to New York, places where there was lots of competition, for sure, but lots of opportunity as well. Palm Springs had open mics and various cabaret venues, for sure, but Billy knew if he really wanted to get somewhere with his voice, he needed to be in a bigger city, where there was more of a chance for things like recording contracts, concert deals, and the kind of exposure he needed to get in the public's fickle eye.

He didn't look at his lack of an owned home or lots of possessions as a disadvantage, but as freedom, the liberty to make of his life what he wanted, when he wanted.

And this bright morning, when the two-week grace period he'd imposed on his and Milt's relationship—whatever it was or would be—was over, he realized that pursuing his dreams didn't have to preclude a relationship with Milt. Maybe Milt would simply come with him. Or maybe, if things were good enough with Milt, perhaps Billy would see that there was something waiting for him here, something that had been staring him in the face all along but that he'd never seen.

Perhaps there was a way he *could* have it all.

Why not? He was only dreaming.

He went through a little mental checklist of all they'd need for their hike today: his CamelBak reservoir, hiking boots, compass, sunscreen, shades, baseball cap, Larabars (in apple pie flavor), and just in case, his trusty snakebite kit. Although he'd only seen one once on a trail, rattlesnakes were always present. It was their turf, not his, and he had to remember that. As long as he did, he believed the two species would get along.

Billy smiled when he had the idea of making up a little hiking package for Milt. He knew Milt, of course, had his own hiking gear, but he threw together a couple of Larabars, an old extra compass he had, a guide to Palm Springs area trails, and a brand-new tube of sunscreen and put them all in a grocery store bag from Ralphs. It was just a gesture, a way of saying he was glad they'd be together today.

He headed out into the morning, hoping to see Milt emerge from his trailer, preceded by Ruby. It was a common enough sight, but it always gave his heart a little lift. Even though he imagined the pair in his mind's eye, he failed to conjure them up.

The morning was bright and still. In the air was a sweet smell that Billy couldn't quite identify but was glad of anyway. A hummingbird, gray and iridescent green, swooped down right before his eyes, its beating wings a blur, before soaring upward again.

He came up the little stone path that led to Milt's back door and paused to look in his window, not to be nosy, but to make sure Milt was actually up and about. It was, after all, only a little after 7:00 a.m. Not everyone in the world shared Billy's fondness for early mornings.

It took his eyes a moment to adjust—as the window itself was almost a mirror, facing the east and the just-risen sun—but when they did, Billy felt like someone had punched him in the gut. He seriously worried for a moment that the eggs, avocado, and salsa he'd had for breakfast might come up. He put a hand to his gut in an attempt to still its churning.

Milt wasn't by himself.

And by that Billy didn't mean the usual—Ruby scampering about his feet, hoping a crumb or two might fall from whatever Milt was eating.

No, Milt, at a little after seven in the morning, was in his kitchen with a man. A very handsome man. Broad-shouldered, powerful, with close-cropped hair and the kind of build one would associate with a linebacker.

Billy's heart sank. His jealousy slammed into place as if it had never gone missing, loosing a storm of angry bees in his head.

They were embracing. Milt was clad only in a pair of blue, gray, and red pajama bottoms. The man wore a white T-shirt that clung to him and a pair of boxer shorts.

Can it be? Maybe it is. This sure as hell looks like a morning-after moment. Billy turned away, feeling a rush of emotions he couldn't or didn't want to identify on this pretty morning so at odds with the sudden turmoil rushing through his entire being. *I don't want to see them kiss. I'd really lose it then.*

He had to plop down suddenly on the pavers, his breathing coming fast, his heart racing. Quickly his mind assembled a story. *He forgot all about the two weeks. The "date," in both respects, slipped from his mind. He moved on, as I knew he would. I just hoped it would be with me. But who can blame him for bringing that hunk home? Maybe it's just a sex thing....* And that thought stoked the nausea back up into high gear, even though the two of them had never done more than hold each other.

Still, to see Milt in another man's arms was sickening, and Billy felt a nearly overwhelming sense of loss. His rational mind tried to tell him it was nothing, a one-nighter and that Milt would be kicking the guy out soon and getting himself ready for their hike.

Milt certainly has no reason to think he's going steady with me. For God's sake, man, get a grip!

Billy wanted to smile at his own folly but couldn't. He slowly got to his feet and brushed off the back of his jeans. He took a quick look over his shoulder. Milt was now at the stove, stirring something in a pan; he was laughing at something the other man said. They looked like quite the happy couple. Milt had yet to cook for him!

How fucking homey.

Billy set down his gifts for Milt on a little side table and started back home.

Life was certainly full of surprises, not all of them pleasant.

Billy was glad there was no alcohol in his trailer. Because a Bloody Mary would taste great right about now.

CHAPTER 15

SUNDAY NIGHT and Milt had just taken Ruby out for her final walk. They'd strolled around the park, stopping at the chain-link fencing for the pool to watch a couple of his younger neighbors, a newly married couple, frolic in the water, the moon stretched oval on its almost navy blue surface. They didn't even notice Milt and Ruby; they were too busy with their horseplay and their kissing. Milt was sure that, even though they were in the relatively cool waters of the pool, fires were being stoked.

He recalled being that young, being that in love—where the only thing that existed was the other, the beating heart of the one you cared so much for that the world around seemed to blur. He wished this couple well and that their period of bliss would endure for a long, long time.

Ruby got down into a crouch, watching the swimmers, every so often emitting a little whine. She loved

the water, and even though it was against the rules, Milt
would, on quiet nights when no one else was around, let
her jump in and paddle around. Sometimes he'd throw
a ball for her and she'd leap from the side of the pool
to catch it and then splash down into the dark water. It
always made him laugh and brought joy to his heart to
see this creature, who'd endured such abuse, so happy.

Tonight, the couple ruined any chance of Ruby
taking a nighttime dip. But it was okay. Ruby might
not agree, but seeing the couple made Milt a little an-
ticipatory. Tomorrow he'd get together with Billy for
the first time after a couple of weeks apart, and he felt
like he was actually now ready for him. He was keeping his options open, because he knew his heart was a
fickle and fragile thing, and it could take him by surprise—either way. It could, for example, release him
from being a perpetual widower and allow him to open
the door to caring for a new man. It might even push
him a little toward Billy, saying, in effect, "Go ahead,
hon, you've waited long enough. You deserve this." Or,
the other side of the coin, it might let him know, once
again, that his heart was bound forever to Corky, just as
he'd promised him so many times over the years and
not just that one time he remembered so well near the
end of his life.

Milt was smart enough to know things could go
either way. And he was old enough to realize that often
our feelings took off in surprising directions, not behaving in the manner we expected them to.

Still, he was excited for the morning to come and
excited to be spending a whole day again with Billy. After the hike he'd already planned what they'd
do: a dip in the pool (*sorry, Ruby, you'll have to stay
home*) and then taking Billy to one of his finds, a little

Vietnamese place he'd discovered in a strip mall on the north end of Palm Canyon, a place called the Rooster and the Pig, that had the freshest and most amazing Vietnamese food Milt had ever eaten, not that he'd had much. Summitville's only nod to Asian cuisine had been a Panda Express on the highway near Walmart—hardly even comparable. Milt wanted to share something *he'd* found on his own in Palm Springs. He hoped Billy wasn't aware yet of the charming little restaurant.

After much tugging and promises to bring her back the following night, late, Milt managed to get Ruby to leave the pool and give up on her dreams of being a sea lion.

At the trailer he refilled her bowl with the filtered water he kept in the fridge and leaned back against the counter to watch with satisfaction as she lapped it up. It was getting on toward nine, and Milt was looking forward to crawling into bed early and turning the TV on. He was currently bingeing on Netflix's reboot of *Queer Eye* and was enjoying the makeovers and even the expert manipulation of his emotions. There hadn't been an episode yet that had failed to elicit a tear or two from him.

"C'mon, girl, you ready to call it a night?" It was a bit earlier than they'd usually retire, but Milt wanted to be well-rested for the hike in the morning.

He'd just finished brushing his teeth when he heard the purr of a car engine through his screened bedroom window. There was the sound of a car door slamming and then footsteps. He glanced over at Ruby, who, like a dutiful wife, had already taken her place on the bed, her head on the pillow next to Milt's. He smiled, shaking his head.

He crossed the room to peer out into the gloom, thinking that it certainly sounded like someone had pulled up in front of his home. But neighbors were very close by in the trailer park, so undoubtedly the car and the footsteps were headed toward someone else. He was expecting no one.

Ruby, taking her cue from him, raised up her head and directed her attention to the open bedroom window. A breeze rustled the curtain.

"Milt?" a figure in the darkness outside asked.

Ruby gave a soft little bark. She hopped down from the bed and clicked to the back door.

Milt peered more closely, squinting. Someone was out there, but because of the way the light hit him, he was little more than a silhouette. A big silhouette, one that looked vaguely familiar.

Could it be?

Milt threw on a T-shirt and some flip-flops and hurried to the back door, which Ruby was pawing. He opened it and Ruby dashed out. He didn't worry about her running away any longer. She knew how good she had it here, and after the flood, Milt had taken considerable care in training her (with lots of cut-up hot dogs) into coming when she was called.

"Ruby! Sit."

Good girl that she was, she dropped down only a foot or so from the visitor. Milt grinned as he realized who it was. Grinned bigger with delight at this nighttime surprise from completely out of the blue.

"My God. You ever hear of phoning first?" Milt picked up the pace and launched himself into the big and bearish arms of his very best friend from Summitville, Ohio, Dane Bernard. The two of them had been chief confidantes and consolers to the other throughout some of their most joyous and most trying life experiences. They'd taught, side by side, for years at Summitville High School.

"And spoil the surprise?" Dane's laugh, like Dane himself, was big and warm. "I needed a break, and I guessed my buddy out here could use a nice surprise. Hope I'm not wrong." He laughed again, booming.

Milt lost himself in Dane's hug. It was very much like being surrounded by a favorite quilt—absolute comfort and security.

After holding each other for a few moments, Milt found the fortitude to break away.

"And who's this?" Dane asked. Ruby was going nuts, whining and circling them, her tail a blur that rivaled hummingbird wings.

"That's Ruby. And I'm not even going to try to, um, curb her enthusiasm." As if she'd heard him, Ruby jumped up on Dane's sizable chest, bouncing off it. Dane laughed and finally squatted down beside her to show her some love.

"She thinks she's who you came to see," Milt said. Ruby had always had an unerring sense when it came to people—who to cozy up to and who to lean away from. Milt trusted her instincts as much, if not more, than his own.

"Who says she isn't?" Dane finished petting and scratching Ruby, stood, and picked up his leather duffel bag. "Seriously. I hope it's okay, me showing up like this. The weather's so shitty back home, in the teens, with snow and sleet that feels like needles. Seth's busy with the school play, and I…." His voice trailed off for a moment, and it was obvious he was caught up in emotion. "And I just missed you so damn much, I thought I needed to get out here and see you. There was a cheap last-minute flight deal. I snatched it up without even questioning."

Milt cocked his head, feeling a little choked up himself. "That's so sweet. I've missed you too, brother."

"And listen, I know this is a surprise, so please feel free to go on about your business while I'm here. No special concessions. Soaking up some sun will be consolation enough for when you're not around. I passed the pool on the way in." Dane took a deep breath of what Milt had come to view as the "chilly" nighttime air and exhaled with a big, pleasure-filled "Ah."

"The good news is my schedule is wide open." Milt did feel a twinge of disappointment that he'd have to include Dane on the hike tomorrow. But Dane was such a lovable man, he was certain Billy would be utterly charmed by him, and the three of them would have a great time. He had plenty of time, he supposed, to be alone with Billy.

"And I don't mind couch-surfing."

"Good thing, because my closet of a guest room is my office." Milt put a guiding hand on Dane's shoulder. "Come on inside. Let's get you a drink and a comfortable place to land."

"I just need to hit the john and set down my bag. Hey! Can we sit out here for a bit?"

"Grab a couple of beers out of the fridge while you're in there." Milt realized he was already getting acclimated to desert heat, because it didn't even cross his mind to sit outside tonight. In the low sixties? Too damn cold! But he'd endure for his Midwestern buddy.

"Will do. Back in a flash."

Milt plopped down in one of the aluminum chairs to wait. Ruby curled up at his feet. He couldn't keep the smile off his face. Life really was often full of the most unexpected surprises. His heart was filled with gladness. This was a gift he'd never expected, but now, Dane being here just felt so right.

He glanced over at Billy's trailer and thought *I've got so much to tell Dane*. Dane had loved Corky too, though, and Milt wondered how he'd take the news of his interest in Billy. Would he see it as a betrayal? *Oh, come on! I'm quite sure you're the only one who sees it that way!*

Dane returned in short order with the beers. He'd even snooped in Milt's cupboards and found a box of Cheez-Its. It was a party!

They sat for a long time, through a couple more beers and lots of catching up. Dane told him all the Summitville news, particularly the gossip that revolved around the high school, and Milt brought Dane up to date on his life here in Palm Springs. He'd gestured toward Billy's trailer with his beer bottle and said, "And that's where Billy lives."

"Oh? And who's Billy?" Dane raised his eyebrows, a grin lifting the corner of his mouth.

And Milt described him in glowing terms—not only his handsome blond looks but his warm heart and caring personality.

"So, you like this guy?" Dane leaned forward a little.

And Milt found himself enduring a stab of guilt. He hated that he was, but hell, there was no denying what he felt. He wished, for the briefest of moments, that he hadn't mentioned Billy at all. It made him a little sad to see the look of anticipation and happiness on Dane's face at the mention of a new man. He could practically read what Dane was thinking—how it was good Milt was finally moving on, how great it would be for him to find someone to replace Corky, to put some salve on the wounds of his loss and grief. Why did that make him feel sad?

"He's nice," Milt said, hiding elaborating behind a couple more swigs of beer and a handful of Cheez-Its. He stretched after swallowing, arms over his head, big yawn. "I don't know about you, but I'm pooped." He reached down to rub the top of Ruby's head. "This one here, she has me up at the crack of dawn."

"Sure, sure." Dane stood and stretched too. Milt was still amazed, after all these years, how big he was—a gentle giant. "Plans for tomorrow?" Dane gathered up their empties and the empty cracker box as well, doing a delicate and competent balancing act.

Milt grinned. "Um, actually, yes, but you can come too. Billy and I are going on a hike. I think we're going to check out one of the trails at Joshua Tree."

They headed inside. "Let me think about it. There's something very appealing about just lounging by the pool all day. I've got the new Stephen King on my Kindle, and I'm picturing myself with something fruity in a big tumbler, just soaking up the rays. I want Seth to be jealous when I come back with a tan."

"Well, you're certainly welcome to join us if you change your mind. Your day doesn't sound half bad either. Surprisingly, I don't do that often enough."

Milt dutifully took the empty box and bottles from Dane and placed them into the bin he'd set up for recycling. When he was done, he gave Dane another hug, planting a kiss on his sandpapery cheek. "I'm so glad you're here. I only wish Seth could have come too."

Dane nearly squeezed the air out of him and then let go, laughing. "Ah, it's good for us to have a little time apart. Good for couples in general."

"Everything okay?"

Dane waved the question away. "Everything's great. Me being away for a few will only make him miss me. And when he misses me, I know I can count on a great homecoming, if you get my drift." He winked.

"Well, give him my love. Not *that* kind of love! But you know what I mean."

"I will. This trip is also a little vetting. Next time I'll bring him and we can stay longer—maybe at one of those clothing-optional gay resorts I read about."

Milt shook his head. "You took a long time to come out, buddy, but when you did, you came crashing out."

Dane had been married to a woman for many years, deep in the closet. He and his new husband, Seth, were now raising Dane's two teenage kids together, a girl and boy, Clarissa and Joey. They were the kind of family everyone aspired to be—easy, close, always there for one another.

"I had a lot of lost time to make up for. Good thing Seth's younger than I am." Dane laughed. "I look forward to meeting this Billy."

"He'll be over in the morning."

"Is he, uh, just a friend? Or is there something more?"

Oh, there's something more, all right. But if ever the phrase "it's complicated" applied to a situation, this is it. Milt was simply too tired to get into everything tonight—his being on the fence, Billy's issues…. "Let's just say there might be some potential. I don't know." Milt yawned. He contemplated asking Dane if it was too soon but held back. What difference did it make what Dane thought? This was his life, for heaven's sakes. He shouldn't let himself be swayed by someone else's opinion, no matter which side Dane came down on. "The bed's calling. I'll get you some sheets and a pillow so you can make up the couch. Feel free to watch TV. I have a Roku, so in addition to regular TV, there's Netflix and Hulu. The sound won't bother me. Or Ruby. We both sleep like rocks."

Dane turned Milt and pushed him gently toward his bedroom. "I'll figure it out. You just go get some sleep."

"You sure? Linens are in—"

"The hall closet. I'll find stuff. Don't worry."

They hugged once more before Milt and Ruby headed into his room.

Milt plopped down on the bed after kicking off his flip-flops. *Life's certainly full of surprises.* He smiled to himself. He hadn't realized how hungry he was for old connections.

The fact that Dane was someone with whom he could talk about Corky was special. Someone who knew Corky made Milt feel even closer to him again.

Maybe I should just cancel the hike? Hang out with Dane at the pool. I can take him for Vietnamese. Milt lay down, rearranging his legs so Ruby could get comfortable against him. *Now, now, that's not progressive thinking. And maybe Dane's making his own way tomorrow because he wants to allow you the freedom to be alone with Billy.*

But how could Dane know Milt wanted—needed—to be alone with Billy? That tomorrow marked the beginning, *maybe*, of something.

Milt turned over, punching the pillow under his head to make it conform. He heard the TV click on in the other room and fell asleep to the opening theme of the old Bea Arthur sitcom, *Maude*. His last thought before drifting off to sleep was that one could find anything on TV these days. It was all there.

WHEN MILT awakened the next morning, Ruby already waited by the door, anxious. Her body was tense, and she stared at him with a kind of pleading in her brown eyes. He glanced at the clock and saw it was already six. He was usually up earlier, five at the latest, to take her outside. The poor thing's bladder was probably ready to burst. Bless her heart, though, for having mastered how to hold it.

Milt hopped from the bed and took her out. He passed Dane, snoring on the couch, as they slipped out the door. The morning air was chilly, and Milt brought up the weather on his phone. Fifty-three degrees.

He looked over at Billy's trailer, but it was all dark. And he realized he couldn't wait to see him.

Ruby finished up and trotted over to him, sat, and looked up. She might as well have spoken. "Daddy, feed me."

They went inside. Dane was still snoring softly on the couch, one leg on the floor, blankets and sheet in a heap next to him. He made the couch look like a tiny love seat. Milt thought maybe he should give him his bed. It would be a good-host thing to do.

But for now all that was necessary was this: lifting the bedding from the floor and gently covering Dane with it. He snorted in thanks and turned, facing the back of the couch. Milt envied him his easy slumber.

He got Ruby her breakfast, tiptoeing around the kitchen, trying to make as little noise as possible.

He returned to the bedroom and plopped down on the bed. The memory of his dream came to him all at once, not in scattered images, unconnected, but whole. He was surprised he hadn't recalled it upon waking. It was as though sitting on the bed caused it to rise up in memory.

CORKY SITS on the bank of the Ohio River, back turned to him. The sky is overcast, a mix of pale gray and white, with an opening in the clouds here and there that allows the blue to come through, like a promise. With the passage of the clouds, the water's surface goes alternately muddy, then sparkling, then back to dullness again.

Milt watches him for a moment, seeing only the back of Corky's head as he stares out at the sluggish brown/green water and the island far off on the horizon that splits the flow. Corky wears an old fishing cap that Milt had once dared to try to throw away. It was ragged, worn to a color that nearly defied description, and tattered around the edges. But Corky loved it, Milt supposed, because it reminded him of his youth and fishing for bluegill from these very shores with his father, now long departed.

He can't see Corky's face, and there's a curious silence to everything. Shouldn't there be birds singing? Insects humming? The relentless lap of the water at the pebbled shoreline? There's nothing. It's as though Milt has gone deaf.

Milt takes a few steps toward Corky, a smile flickering on his lips as he anticipates surprising him. Even in a dream, he wonders if this is a figment of his subconscious or if Corky is paying him a visit.

"Sweetie?" he tries to say, but even though he opens his mouth, no sound emerges. His hands flutter uselessly before him.

He plods across the beach, stepping over a piece of driftwood that reminds him of palm tree bark, and ends up just in front of Corky, ostensibly blocking his view of the water and the island.

But here's the horror. It sends a jolt of electricity through Milt.

When he steps in front of Corky, he doesn't see his face, but only the back of his head. Again. He moves around to the other side and is once again confronted with the back of Corky.

He circles around him, feeling a fluttering terror in his gut. No matter from which angle he stands, Corky remains resolutely facing away.

MILT SHOOK his head, feeling a little of the shock and fear the dream had inspired.

What does it mean? he wondered. And a voice, familiar, yet unlike his own, answered him back. *"You know what it means. You just don't understand it yet."*

Disturbed, Milt rose from the bed. He'd heard the toilet flush. Dane was up. To take his mind off things, he'd make them both a big breakfast.

As he left the bedroom, he glanced behind himself, almost expecting to see Corky sitting on the bed, facing away.

But the room was empty.

Dane was just coming out of the bathroom. He eyed Milt. "You've firmed up a bit. You look good."

Heat rose to Milt's cheeks. He realized he was standing there in only his pajama bottoms. He was used to not caring about what he did or didn't wear around the trailer. After all, there was usually no one to see him, save for Ruby. "Thanks."

"You working out?"

"Lots of hiking."

"Well, it looks great on you."

"Ah…." Milt waved the remark away. He noted that Dane was clad only in a T-shirt and boxers, and if anything, his friend had actually put on a few pounds. But when you had a big frame like Dane's, it was very forgiving. He still looked good.

Milt debated whether to go in and put a little more on, but why? They were old friends. They were like brothers. It didn't matter.

"What do you want for breakfast?"

"Oh, you don't have to go to any trouble. I usually just have toast and coffee."

"Please. I'm thrilled you're here. Let me spoil you a little."

"Well, if I remember right, you did make some awesome scrambled eggs."

"I still do. My secret is low and slow." He grinned. "It'll take a while. If you want to grab a shower while I get things started, go ahead. You need time-lapse photography to see my eggs go from liquid to curds, but that's just what makes them so creamy."

"Okay. Done. I know you don't want me spying on your secret technique."

"Right. That's it. Get out of here."

Milt watched him walk away. When he heard the water running, he pulled eggs and half-and-half out of the fridge, along with a block of sharp cheddar and some green onions. Company eggs this morning. He'd make a whole dozen, in case Billy showed up with an appetite.

Just as he was cracking eggs into the pale blue bowl he'd had forever, Dane slipped back into the room. He spun Milt around and engulfed him in a big bear hug. "God, man, I sure have missed you. I keep imagining you'll give up on this California dream and come home to us." He squeezed him tighter, and Milt realized maybe Dane was crying, just a little bit. "But now that I see how beautiful it is here and the potential you have for a new life, well…." He let the phrase trail off as he pulled back to hold Milt at arm's length, to look him in the eye. "Well, brother, I'm happy for you."

Milt wasn't sure what to say. He wondered internally *Do I have a new life? Is there really potential?* He smiled at his friend because he realized, quite suddenly, that he did and there was. "Yeah, I moved to paradise. But that doesn't mean I miss you any less. Nor does it mean," Milt hastened to add, "that I forgot about Corky."

Dane drew him close again, practically squeezing the life out of him, but it was wonderful anyway. In Milt's ear Dane said, "No one thinks that. We'll always know how much you loved Corky. We all did. Moving on, loving again? Sorry, man, but that doesn't mean you didn't love Corky. Do you really think he'd want you to throw away your life just because he's gone?"

And Milt squeezed him back, knowing that Dane had said exactly the right words. True words.

CHAPTER 16

BILLY STOOD outside Cinq, one of the trendy restaurants lining Palm Canyon Drive in Palm Springs' downtown. He'd been debating whether he should go inside or not for the last fifteen minutes.

Why debate? Because, for one, he knew he was standing Milt up. He pictured him looking out his window, waiting for Billy to come up the walkway. Checking the time. Again. Wondering why his friend had not shown up.

And then he'd see him in the arms of *that guy* and get furious all over again, even though he knew he had no right. But jealousy, as Billy had learned again and again over the course of his relatively short life, was not reasonable. One could never "talk through" jealousy. That green-eyed emotion always had its own agenda and was as stubborn as all get-out.

The other reason for his internal debate—and standing out here on the sidewalk like some derelict—was he knew what was inside. Temptation. Ruination. Turning away from his higher power.

Vodka.

Once upon a time, Billy had loved nothing more than a good Bloody Mary. He'd been something of an aficionado, before he'd gotten to the point where drinking became all about the quickness and ease of administration over minor details like taste. But back before drinking became a problem (and if he was being honest, he knew deep down that drinking was *always* a problem), he'd reveled in concocting the perfect one—rich with a good tomato juice (Spicy V8 was his favorite) and amped up with fresh horseradish, Worcestershire sauce, Tabasco, celery salt, and lots of fresh-ground black pepper on the rim. A celery stick and maybe an olive or a pickled vegetable rounded things out—perfection.

Billy knew, anecdotally, that Cinq, a Palm Springs institution with its hip midcentury modern décor in orange and silver, served the best Bloody in town.

And Billy had gotten the idea in his head to drown his sorrows and jealousy in *just one* perfect Bloody Mary.

The reason he didn't go inside, sit himself down, and order what he was certain would be delicious and horribly overpriced, was one of the AA slogans he'd learned in recovery, one he'd committed to memory.

One is too many, a thousand is never enough.

In his heart of hearts, he knew himself well enough to know he wouldn't, couldn't, stop at one. Or two, or even three. No, he'd keep going until he became ugly, angry, maudlin, and was asked, politely—at least at first—to leave the premises.

He'd seen this particular movie so many times, he knew its plot and ending by heart.

Billy sighed and walked down the street a bit. He fished his phone out of his hip pocket. He had a sponsor here in town, a woman named Eliza, who was great, strict, and loving all at once, with years of her own drunken binges to make her both compassionate and forgiving. And no-bullshit. She knew all the lies. All the deception. All the rationalization.

And she tolerated none of it.

But this morning called for someone else—his old sponsor, Jon, back in Chicago.

Jon picked up on the first ring. "What's going on?" No hello. No long time no hear. No easy pleasantries. That was his Jon McGregor, always direct. Always to the point. It's what Billy both loved and hated about him.

And Billy knew no how do you dos were needed here, even though it had been over two years since he'd spoken to Jon. "Thinkin' about having a Bloody Mary this fine Southern California morning."

"Hang on."

Billy heard him lighting a cigarette, the friction of the lighter, the snap of it closing—the long exhalation after. He could almost smell the smoke. It made him long for one. *Hey! There's a gas station just a couple blocks north. You can grab a pack there. Smoke a couple and then throw the pack away. Nobody has to know.* Billy let the thought ricochet around a bit, a silly grin pulling up the corners of his lips. And then he thought *Shut up!* He'd given up the smokes along with the drinking a long time ago, but sometimes a craving could hit him with the same intensity as though he'd just quit yesterday. Now was one of those times. The addict in him never really left.

He knew cigarettes were a trigger, a big one. Lighting up was almost always followed by pouring alcohol down his throat. His was not to question why, only to avoid it.

On another exhale, Jon asked, "You are?"

"Yeah." Billy could already feel the urge, so fierce only a second ago, begin to evaporate like a cloud of smoke. Amazing what simply reaching out could do.

"Why?"

And Billy told him the truth—how he'd fallen for Milt, their uneasy dance of attraction and friendship, the hot guy in Milt's arms this morning.

"And you think pouring some vodka and tomato juice down your gullet will solve your problem? Make that jealousy disappear just like that?" Jon snapped his fingers.

"For the time being." Billy's answer, he thought, was honest.

"Uh-huh." Jon drew in on his cigarette, blew out smoke, and Billy wondered if he was actually trying to drive him crazy. If he was, he was succeeding. Jon said, "Maybe it will. For a bit. Vodka can blot out a lot. But hey, gotta ask you, brother—you think those problems will still be there after you get one, two, three, or more bloodies in you?"

Billy watched a couple of guys in a vintage teal Corvette convertible cruise by, sunglasses in place, top down even though it was too cold for it. He knew the answer, knew he didn't even need to say it.

Instead he said, "No matter what," another AA slogan. "Don't drink—no matter what."

"Right."

"Right." Billy laughed, started adding more distance between himself and the restaurant. "Why do you have to spoil all my fun, Jon?"

"Because I can." Jon's chuckle was deep, throaty, and it ended in a cough.

Billy knew better than to suggest he quit smoking. AA was rife with smokers; it seemed to be the one addiction most of them couldn't give up. If Billy thought for a minute he could still smoke and not drink, he'd do it. Lungs and singing voice be damned.

"And because you know I want you to," Billy confessed.

"That too. So, other than this current crisis, how you doin'?"

WHEN BILLY got home, he felt relieved. Relieved he didn't drink. Didn't smoke. Didn't throw away years of sobriety with one swallow. Man, what a brain-dead move that would have been. He actually got down on his knees in a shaft of sunlight next to his bed to thank his higher power, who he believed showed up in the form of Jon, for saving him once again. One thing he knew, even if he didn't quite understand who or what his higher power was—it was always there for him; he only needed to accept its help.

That knowledge was a saving grace of Billy's life.

Yet he still didn't feel better about Milt. He stood and glanced out his window and was ticked that the guy was still there, sitting on the patio, drinking a goddamn beer. He was big. Good-looking too, the kind of beefy man that once upon a time had graced movies and magazines Billy had seen from Colt Studio. In a second of low self-esteem, Billy thought there was no competing with the hunk across the way, sitting there with his shirt off.

Who said there was a competition? And even if there was, why did it matter who won? You're making this into something it's not. Surrender. Serenity. Let go and let God. Blah, blah, blah.

Billy glanced down at his phone. Milt had texted and called dozens of times. Billy felt a twinge of guilt. He also felt a twinge of shame and embarrassment. He was being silly. He was thinking little of himself.

If Milt was so wrapped up in this hunky guy at his place, would he have been texting and calling Billy over and over again? Was that really the behavior of an infatuated man? *Maybe the infatuation is for* you, *dumbass. Just look at your damn phone to see the proof.*

But he couldn't talk to Milt. Whether the man sitting in his yard right now was a relative, a friend, a one-night stand who didn't know when to leave, or a new boyfriend didn't matter. Billy wasn't ready—emotionally—to have it out with Milt. Not yet. He wasn't prepared for the truth, no matter what it turned out to be.

So he shut off his phone and threw it on the kitchen counter next to the toaster.

He grabbed a little can of V8 from his minifridge, and then sat down at his breakfast nook to stare out the window. This side of the trailer faced west toward San Jacinto. Billy gazed up at its gray/brown peaks, capped with pine trees and other desert vegetation, and simply let their immortal Zen-like strength seep into him. The mountains had a kind of power, Billy believed, that couldn't be put into words. But sometimes he could feel that power, when he loosened up his monkey mind and his ego to let it seep in.

Now was one of those times, and Billy kind of drifted as he imagined the top of the mountain. He'd gone up via the Palm Springs aerial tramway many times, hiked around its shady forest and reveled in its coolness and stunning panoramas.

When at last he descended from his mental journey, he finished off the V8 and got himself a pen and a pad of paper he kept in one of the kitchen drawers. He used these only for grocery store lists, but today he thought he'd do something out of the ordinary—write a letter. Who wrote letters these days? Practically no one. But Billy felt the occasion called for something more solid than the ephemera of an email.

Dear Milt,

I care about you. I care a lot. You came into my life in the summer, and I watched as you struggled to move in, to get settled. I watched as you brought Ruby home and saw your joy in your new companion. That joy floated over and filled me up too, even if I was a little jealous of her and all the attention you showered on her. I wanted some too! LOL.

I watched and waited, hoping for a chance to meet. I made eye contact. I said hello dozens of times. Remember? I tried to chat with you about the weather, about the temperature of the pool, the big pothole near the entrance, where you were from.

But you were having none of it.

I couldn't get even a little close until the day of that summer storm. The flood! Oh God, it was terrible, wasn't it?

Except it wasn't. I look at that rare windy deluge as a blessing because it was my entree into your life. One thing I learned, big lesson, in AA was that we have to give in order to receive. Reaching out to you that day, I know I made a friend.

And maybe that's all I made, despite my wishes to the contrary. I'm just going to lay my truth out here on the line, Milt. I've always been, I think, a bit of an empath. It's my gift and my curse. But it lets me know, right away, before I have any logical reason for knowing, who's right for me and who's not. That feeling is pretty much infallible.

And I knew you were right for me.

You are right for me. I can say that with certainty. Whether I'm right for you is a question only you can answer. When you know. When you're ready. And I surrender to the thought that you may decide you're never ready for me, not in the way I dream of.

I wish I could say that's okay. For the best part of me, the spirit side of me, it is okay. But I wear this suit of human clothes around, and it's tattered and worn-out at the elbows and knees. It clings to fantasies like true love and soul mates.

Ah, I'm going off on a tangent here. I just wanted you to know that I care.

And that I hurt.

I saw you with that guy. You know the guy. The big lug in your kitchen, the one you were hugging and making breakfast for. It's none of my business—it pains me to say that.

I don't even know what he is to you. And my self-doubting, low-self-esteem self wants to make me believe he's the light of the world, the answer to your prayers. My head tells me he could be nothing more than a cousin, a buddy from your past, or an online hookup that spilled over into the morning. That last part gives me a twinge that hurts as bad as you kicking me in the balls. And the bottom line really is: it's none of my damn business.

Not fair of me to lay this at your innocent feet, I know.

And I don't know where I'm going with this.

Yeah, I do.

And Billy stopped writing. He stared down at the letter, read it over once, twice. And then he picked it up and tore it into pieces. He dropped the scraps of paper into the trash can.

He kind of believed and kind of didn't that he set out with the intention that he'd never give Milt the letter, but part of him wanted to. Just so Milt could see what he was missing out on. So maybe Milt would feel bad for making him feel bad.

Billy knew those motivations were simply him being childish. Being selfish. Self-seeking, as they said in the twelve-step rooms. See, giving Milt the letter would place a responsibility on him that didn't belong to him. That responsibility was Billy's and Billy's alone.

Billy knew what he had to do. He had to go over there and *talk* to Milt. And yes, he needed to apologize for not showing up when they'd made plans.

It was the right thing, the decent thing to do.

Billy hurried to shower, shave, and make himself presentable.

And then he set off into the afternoon sun to make amends, whether the recipient of those amends knew he needed them or not. Billy needed to make them to try to set things right in his world again.

But Milt wasn't home. Or at least he wasn't answering the door.

The trailer was empty. Billy peered into the windows. Nobody home. No dog, no extra man, no Milt.

Billy started back home. "Serves you right, you big fool. They probably went without you."

JUST AS he reached his door, he heard a car engine and turned to see Milt, Ruby, and that damn guy, Mr.

Hunkalicious, pulling into Milt's driveway. Even from this distance, he could see the quizzical look Milt gave him. Billy picked up on the telepathy quite readily. Milt was broadcasting "Where the hell were you?"

Billy stood near his door, a little helpless, knowing the grin he shot back at Milt was sheepish. A part of him simply wanted to slip inside.

But he forced himself to stay put, watching as the three of them emerged from the car. He knew all three were staring at him, but he didn't allow it to bother him. If he was being honest, he'd have to admit this situation was actually kind of funny.

Billy took in a deep breath and crossed the space that separated them. He had his priorities straight. First, he squatted down to give Ruby some love, because she was going nuts. Second, he straightened up, smiled at the big guy, and extended his hand. "Hi, I'm Billy Blue. I live next door." It took all his strength to not ask who the guy was. Again, it was none of his business. If Milt, or the guy himself, wanted to let him know, they would.

The guy, as Billy expected, had a killer handshake. Billy had to refrain from saying "Ow" and shaking out his own hand afterward. Alpha-male posturing? He wondered.

"I'm Dane Bernard."

Milt stepped up, eyeing Billy curiously. He patted Dane's shoulder. "Dane's one of my oldest and dearest friends from back in Ohio. He came out for a long weekend as a surprise to me."

Billy sighed with relief. Dane wasn't a lover, a hookup, or anything of that order, but only a good friend. Billy also felt like kicking himself. Why didn't he allow for that possibility first? Why had he let his mind cloud up with jealousy?

Because you care. Give yourself a break.

"It's good to meet you, Dane." Billy gave him a big smile, not only to welcome Dane, but also because he was now capable. The clouds had lifted, and the sky was once again a clear and sunny blue. Even though it wasn't true, Billy added, "Milt's told me all about you. He speaks very highly of you."

"I do?" Milt gave Dane a look, and they both burst into laughter.

"You do," Dane said. "Of course you do. What else could you say? Everyone speaks very highly of me." He turned back to Billy. "And Milt speaks very highly of you too, Billy. In fact, I think he might have a little crush." He winked at Milt. "So watch out."

It was a small delight to Billy to see the flush redden Milt's cheeks. He glared at Dane, shaking his head.

Billy wanted to immediately quiz Milt. "A crush? Really? You do?" but he held all the queries inside. He could see Milt was embarrassed, bordering on humiliated. If he didn't have such a stake in this game, he would have thought the situation laugh-out-loud funny.

Instead, mercifully, he changed the subject. It was time to make amends. Billy drew in a breath and then just came out with it. He clasped Milt's shoulder. "Hey, man, I'm really sorry I didn't show this morning. I wish I had some good excuse to give, but I don't, other than me being an ass. Therefore, I apologize. I hope you can forgive me."

Billy didn't need to be an empath to read the hurt and confusion on Milt's face. He knew Milt probably wondered why he'd stood him up without a good reason to explain it.

"It's so unlike you," Milt said softly. "Is everything okay?"

Billy eyed Dane, silently pleading for a moment alone. If he didn't catch on in a second, Billy would break down and ask him for this small grace.

But Dane, bless his heart, got why Billy was staring pointedly at him. Or at least that's what Billy deduced.

Dane said, "I need to go inside, boys." He winked. "Come on, Ruby." He tapped his thigh, and she dutifully followed. Once both man and beast had gone inside with the door closed behind them, Billy turned back to Milt and said, "Yeah, everything's okay. Except I'm an idiot. A jealous fool. A dick." Billy chuckled. *Could I tell him the truth? Yes, I can. And I will. Remember the tenth step? When you're wrong, buddy, you promptly admit it.* So he spilled the beans, told Milt how he'd been a Peeping Tom that morning and got more than an eyeful. "An eyeful I of course completely misinterpreted." Billy smiled. "I'm sorry."

"You were jealous?" Milt was grinning. "Really? Dane's like my brother. Or my sister, if the mood's right." He chuckled. "If you saw anything even remotely sexual between us, you were way off. That would be like incest." Milt rubbed the toe of his shoe in the dust at his feet. "But I have to admit—I'm flattered."

"You are?"

"Yeah, hell yeah. It's been a long time since I inspired jealousy in anyone. I've been an old married guy for so long such stuff doesn't even cross my mind." He smiled. "You do an old man's heart good."

"Shut up," Billy said. "You're hardly an old man. And I bet, even when you were married, you inspired lots of jealousy, whether you knew it or not."

"Well, I don't know about that. And I'm sorry for the confusion. If you'd just knocked on the door, we could have avoided all of it."

"Believe me, I know. I know. I have a child's mind sometimes."

"Don't be so hard on yourself," Milt said. "You're only human."

Billy didn't argue. He just nodded.

Neither of them said anything for a few moments. Both turned to look as they heard the back door of the trailer opening.

Milt said, "It's just too bad. I was looking forward to our hike."

"So was I. Believe me. More than you know."

"Hey. I was gonna take Dane out for dinner. I was thinking Vietnamese. You want to join us?"

And Billy did. More than anything. But he thought a little self-sacrifice was called for here, so he said, "No. That's okay. You enjoy your friend. He's only here for the weekend, right?"

"Yeah, but—"

Billy held up a hand. "Don't. It's okay. I'm sure you guys have lots of catching up to do." He didn't say it, but he knew they'd most likely want to talk about Corky. "I'll just let you guys do your thing. When Dane goes back, you'll be in touch, I hope, and we can re-schedule that hike. The trails aren't going anywhere."

Milt looked at him curiously and then, Billy thought, with gratitude. "Okay. Talk soon." And he leaned forward and planted a small kiss on Billy's face. It landed just north of his upper lip. It should have been awkward, but what it was was wonderful. When he stepped back, Billy had the pleasure of seeing that ridge of rose emerge across Milt's cheeks again.

"Later, tater."

Billy watched him walk away.

He waved a hand and went home.

CHAPTER 17

IT WAS the last night of Dane's stay. He was due to get up early in the morning to catch his flight back to Pittsburgh. Since Dane would need to leave no later than 4:00 a.m., Milt had planned an early dinner in. He'd made his old reliable—baked ziti with meat sauce and ricotta. There was some garlic bread and a peppery salad of arugula and tomatoes in a lemon vinaigrette.

They'd drunk a lot of red wine, an exceptional California Syrah, with their meal, and now they sat at Milt's little kitchen table, a little drowsy, maybe a little drunk. Conversation was drifting, as it sometimes does when liberated by the grape, toward the personal.

Milt felt more introspective, and perhaps just a touch maudlin, than he had all weekend. He and Dane had done the usual touristy stuff—visiting downtown Palm Springs and checking out things like the art galleries, shops, and the Hollywood-style stars on the sidewalk. They'd hiked the Araby Trail and ogled Bob

Hope's futuristic-looking old mansion tucked into the side of the mountain. They'd driven out to Rancho Mirage and dined in the old-school kitschy elegance of Lord Fletcher's.

What they hadn't done much of was talk—heart-to-heart.

Milt gazed at Dane, his oldest and best friend, across the table, sad that in just a few hours he'd be on an eastbound plane, headed home to Seth and Summitville. Milt knew just the life he'd be returning to. In his mind's eye, he could see the white brick high school at the top of the hill where both of them had worked together for so many years, commiserating over and celebrating both the failures and successes of their respective students. He reveled in the view of the foothills of the Appalachians, which surrounded their little town. That view, from above, also afforded him a peek at the Ohio River as it curved, serpentine, through the little town. For a moment Milt felt almost as though he were back there—he knew its streets so well.

Milt found himself missing Dane already. Who knew when he'd come back? For a few days Dane brought the old connections alive. Milt realized those connections were based in the heart and not in geography, because when he was with Dane, it was as though no time at all had passed. That, Milt thought, was the measure of true friendship.

Dane had brought a piece of home with him. He'd brought the *peace* of home with him, making Milt realize how much he'd missed home—as he still thought of Summitville.

"I miss it."

Dane immediately caught on. "Home?" His face lit up. "You think you might want to come back?"

Milt swirled the wine in his glass, staring down at its deep red hue, watching as the swirling slowed, leaving legs behind. For just a moment, perhaps, there was a pull toward Ohio. He *could* return. He could do anything he wanted, really, couldn't he? It would wipe out what little money he had left, but he could do it. Really, it wouldn't even be that much trouble.

Returning to the little town on the banks of the Ohio River meant he could start right back up where he'd left off with his old friends there. He could buy another house, probably smaller and with not as pretty of a view as the one he'd shared with Corky, but real estate back in Summitville was dirt cheap. A decent two-bedroom home in a perfectly acceptable neighborhood could be had for well under a hundred thousand dollars.

He could find a job. Something—even a greeter at Walmart. Or maybe something would open up at the high school for him. His years of teaching there should count for something, right? Even if he was just a teacher's assistant, it would be okay. Milt had never been proud.

He had a quick glimpse of himself twenty or thirty years into the future, sitting on a porch swing, clutching a mug of beer. Dappled shadows would make patterns of late-afternoon summer light across his face. The newspaper, folded so he could do the crossword puzzle, would lay beside him. At his feet, a dog as old and tired as he was, curled up and snoring.

It was comforting, in a way. And sad. Because, other than the dog, he was alone.

Just like he was now.

But at least here, in the desert, he had the potential of a new life, one that was more vibrant than sedate. Sometimes life was about embracing risk over comfort.

Home, he'd revel in his memories—of Corky, of course, but also of his mother, passed from cancer seven years ago, and his poor dad, whom a heart attack had taken so early, at age fifty-five. He could walk the banks of the Ohio, recalling the days of his boyhood there, skipping stones and seeing what the river washed up. In the summer he'd swim covertly in its greenish-brown waters, avoiding the currents his mom always warned would surely drag him under.

He could attend the Christmas parade downtown, the Fourth of July fireworks up the river near Pittsburgh, the school plays, and the summer carnivals.

It would be easy. Like getting on a bicycle after not having ridden one for a long, long while.

"No." Milt smiled across the table at Dane. "This is where I am now. My blood's gotten acclimated to the heat. I have Ruby." He looked over at the dog, curled up in her bed in a corner of the living room. Her ears perked up when Milt mentioned her name, but she didn't stir. She'd been made sleepy, heavy, by being slipped meat and pasta at the table earlier.

"And there's more possibility for me here now. You know?" Milt surprised himself. He honestly couldn't have predicted he'd be voicing these words, these sentiments. But now that they were tumbling from his lips, almost as though he'd rehearsed them, he realized they were true.

"I spent a long time living for someone else. Don't get me wrong—I don't begrudge Corky that time. I cared for him because I loved him with all my heart. I still do. I did it because I know, without even the smallest bit of doubt, that if the tables were turned, he'd have done the exact same thing for me. Caring for my sick and dying husband was both a horror and a joy, a blessing. I'm grateful to have been his person, to have been there for him when he most needed me, whether he knew it or not."

Milt had to stop. The tears were welling in his eyes, the lump in his throat expanding. Dane, in his wisdom, didn't say anything stupid. He didn't say anything at all. He merely reached across the table and took Milt's hand and squeezed it.

He let go when Milt found himself capable of going on. "It's taken me these months out here—alone—to realize that Corky loved me so much he would want this new life for me." Milt smiled through his tears. He confessed, "I think he's even let me know it—in subtle little ways."

"It *is* beautiful here," Dane said quietly.

"You're disappointed, aren't you?" Milt cocked his head. He poured them both some more wine. "The truth is, Dane, if you'd have come out here a few months sooner, I might have actually packed things up and come back with you." Milt drained his wineglass. "But things have changed." Milt smiled. "You really thought you might lure me back?"

"Well, I'd be lying if I said I came out here only as a getaway, although I did desperately need some Milt time *and* some sun!" He chuckled. "But before I left, Seth and I talked about it. There was this hope, and I'll be the first to admit it was a very selfish hope, that I'd come out here and find you feeling a little lost and a lot homesick. And through careful, subtle persuasion, my specialty, I'd talk you into coming back. Seth even said to offer our place as a landing pad until you could get yourself back together—as we both knew you would.

"So when you said you missed it, I leaped on that, because I wasn't sure you did." He smiled, but there was a little sadness there. "I could see you were making your way here. I could see a certain settling in. I never expected to see you in a trailer, for Christ's sake, but it's cute, and it's homey, and it's *you*. Yours alone. And I see that as healthy. I see that as a good thing, as much as the selfish part of me wants you miserable, pining for the cold and gray skies of eastern Ohio. Ha! Fat chance.

"No, Milt, my old buddy. I see good things for you here." Dane's gaze drifted out the window, and Milt imagined he was looking at Billy's trailer.

Dane said, "You didn't ask, and you sure as hell don't need it, but you have my blessing." He looked toward the silver trailer outside again. "You deserve something for yourself. And I know Corky would be as happy for you as I am. As happy as Seth will be when I tell him all about this Billy Blue person." Dane burst into laughter. "That's *not* his real name, is it?"

Milt laughed. Nothing was funny, but there was a sense of joy bubbling over. "Yes. It's his real name. Least as far as I know. He makes me think of these impossible expanses of blue skies we get out here. He makes me hopeful. I just might be falling in love." Milt's gaze went quickly down to the surface of the kitchen table. *Where did that come from?*

Dane stood up. He crossed to Milt and bent down to hug him. "Your hope, I'm sure, isn't misplaced." He squeezed Milt a little harder, that way he had, bordering on painful, and then straightened up. "Since you did all the cooking, why don't you let me clean up and take Miss Ruby out for her final walk?"

"You don't have to do that—" Milt started to protest.

"Milt, Milt, Milt. You don't get it. I'm trying to get rid of you. I need to get to bed. Now, it'll take me ten minutes to load up the dishwasher and watch your pup pee. Would you just go so I can *also* get the couch made up?"

"Got it." Milt stood, gave Dane a lingering full-body hug. It felt good, real, and right.

He went off to his bedroom.

CHAPTER 18

BILLY REALIZED he wasn't sure. Jesus, when would life, and the decisions we needed to make, ever become simple? Uncomplicated? When he was a kid, Billy had thought that growing up meant knowing what you wanted, how to get it, and exactly what road to travel for happiness. Now he thought the older he got, the more confusing things became.

Milt was right for him.

Milt was wrong for him.

The time for true love was now… or never.

Billy sat in the 7:00 a.m. AA meeting at Sunny Dunes. This meeting was especially for the LGBT people, and Billy attended almost every day because it made for a good start. Apparently a lot of other people felt the same way, because the room was usually packed with between fifty to a hundred people.

Maybe it was due to the early morning light and the promise a new day held, but Billy loved this meeting particularly because it was so friendly. There was always a greeter outside (and Billy had been coming to this meeting long enough that he usually knew the designated greeter, but even if he didn't, it was always nice to be hugged), making each and every person who came into the room feel welcome, whether he or she was there for the first time or had been coming for years.

Inside, it often felt like a family reunion, with lots of laughter, chatting, and more hugs. The big room had become as familiar and as comfortable as his own home. Once upon a time, before he was in the program, Billy would never have imagined an AA meeting could be so friendly, so full of life and fellowship.

But he knew that for many of the people gathered here, and for him, this was a new life. And for many of them, their only life. Why shouldn't it be fun? Why shouldn't it feel special, warm, inclusive? Sobriety didn't have to mean, Jon McGregor once told him, that one had to be sober, not in the strictest sense of the word. We could feel happy and whole if only we'd accept the gifts and miracles that were ours to claim if we simply followed what the program laid out—honesty, openness, willingness.

Because the meeting was so large, Billy didn't always get to share, nor did he always want to. But today he wanted to make sure the meeting's leader that morning noticed his raised hand.

He had something to say.

It took three tries, but finally Billy got called upon. He'd been worried as he watched the clock edge toward eight.

"Good morning! I'm grateful to be here today among all of you guys. Thanks for the lead, Brian, and

congrats to everybody who took chips. You're awesome." Billy stared down at the black Cons he wore,
realizing time was wasting.

"Guys. I've fallen in love." When Billy said the
words, he drew in a sudden breath. In that little space,
several people applauded, and a couple said, "Uh-oh."

"And the good news is he's a great guy. Handsome.
Charming. Loves animals. Sweet as all get-out. So-so
cook. Can't carry a tune in a bucket. But a keeper, I
think, in just about anyone's book." Billy sighed.

"And he's a normie." *Normie* was what people in
the program called those who *didn't* suffer from the disease of addiction/alcoholism. Normies had never been
in recovery, because they'd never needed to. Normies
didn't use buzz words and phrases like "easy does it,"
"let go and let God," "progress, not perfection," "higher power," or "character defects." Normies could go out
to El Portal in Cathedral City and have a margarita or
two with their enchiladas. They could have a Bloody
Mary at brunch at Spencer's. Enjoy a beer on a hot day.
All with no problems, all with no worries that one sip
could lead to a thousand.

Normies really didn't "get" what recovery was all
about. And why should they? It wasn't a part of their world.

When Billy mentioned that his new love interest
was a normie, a groan went up in the room, which
wasn't the reaction Billy had hoped for. Where was that
applause when he needed it?

"Anyway, he knows my past. He knows I'm in recovery. He knows I go to meetings." Billy held back
that "he" had followed him to a meeting once. No need
to dwell on stalkerish stuff like that.

"I think he accepts who I am. A drunk." *But does
he?* Billy wondered. The subject of Billy's disease had

not come up for serious discussion. Not really. "But he knows about my clean time. He knows I love the program and that I love you guys.

"Here's the problem. I worry that, if things progress and get serious, it'll be weird. Like, maybe he'll expect me to stop coming to meetings. Or he'll be jealous of the friends I have in the program. And believe me, kids, when I say there's no way I'd subject some of you to him." There was hooting and laughter. "Just sayin'. See? You get me. I can say that to you and you understand. I can tell you about the bender I went on and how three Chicago police cars chased me home. We can laugh about that. I can talk about being passed out on the floor of the men's room of a movie theater and we can have ourselves a righteous chuckle.

"Him? Maybe not so much. He might not find things like that amusing. He might be put off, or worse, disgusted.

"And I can't blame him for that." Billy sighed, stretching out his legs in front of him.

"What if we don't have common ground? What if it all goes to shit because we're not on the same page?"

Billy looked around. There was a mix of boredom, concern, apathy, and sympathy. Cross talk, or answering questions and offering opinions, was forbidden at meetings, so Billy didn't really expect anything more than what was in front of him right here and right now.

"Anyway, that's all I got. Thanks for listening."

Brian, a heavy guy with a mass of wild white hair, had led the meeting. He thanked Billy for his share and then said they were all out of time. He asked the group to recite the seventh step prayer together. It asked the higher power to accept the good and the bad in each of them—and asked for strength as they went out into the day.

Billy wanted to ask Milt to do the same. He usually felt better after a share, kind of relieved, but today, he just felt more confused.

OUTSIDE IN the parking lot, Billy paused from unlocking his bike when he heard a soft voice behind him calling his name.

He turned to see a woman who'd sat quietly in the back of the room. She was older, maybe fifties, with dyed red hair and a lanky and tall body. A smattering of freckles spread, like a constellation, across the bridge of her nose and her cheeks. When she smiled, she revealed a big gap between her front teeth. In spite of what some might call "defects," Billy thought she was arresting, maybe even stunningly beautiful. Her wide green eyes regarded him with what Billy perceived as amusement.

He stood and extended his hand. "Hey."

"Hi. I'm Char." She looked at the bike and then back at him. "I liked your share."

"You did? Thanks." Billy affixed his bike lock to its proper place on his bicycle. He stood up straighter and moved toward Char. "Why?"

"Because I've been there." She grinned and held up her left hand. With her right hand, she pointed to the simple gold band on her third finger. "Going on ten years now."

"That's great," Billy said. "Happy?"

"Happiness is a fleeting thing. It comes and goes. But we're solid. And… she's a normie. In fact, this woman has a beer and it's lampshade on her head time. She's such a normie that she thinks alcoholics' lives are like Lee Remick and Jack Lemmon in that old flick, *Days of Wine and Roses*. Ever see that one?"

"Oh yeah. Watched it with my sponsor once upon a time, to tell you the truth. I thought it was terrific—and rang true."

"I guess you're right. What I meant was it took me a while to convince Bridget, that's the wife, that we're not all like Lee Remick. Some of us are Jack Lemmon—we do recover."

Billy nodded, remembering how Lee Remick's character in the movie never could manage sobriety—and that factor was what led to the death of their love.

"My point is a relationship between someone in the program and a normie *can* work. It's all about wanting it to." Char looked faraway. "I guess that's true for any relationship. Once you get past the initial 'perfection' stage, it's all about a decision to make it work, huh?"

Billy nodded.

Char went on. "But you guys have to have common ground. You need to understand each other and what makes your relationship unique—its challenges. First and foremost, in my opinion, the normie has to be humble enough and loving enough to know that, for us, sobriety has to come first. Not our spouses. Sorry. Not our jobs, pets, kids. I know that sounds harsh, man, but I think you know what I'm sayin' and why. If we let our sobriety take a back seat to *anything* else, we run the risk of letting our disease become active again—and you know as well as I do that can be a life-or-death thing. Unless we're clean, we're not much good to spouses, employers, pets, or even kids. We have to guard that."

"Yeah. I get that," Billy said. "Only I'm worried that he won't. That he'll feel slighted when I'm off to yet another meeting. Or I'm meeting, say, well, *you* for coffee someday and he wants to come and I tell him no."

"I know," Char said. "And I'm not saying it's easy. Hell, Bridge and I are still negotiating. We still have our differences. She still feels slighted sometimes, even accuses me of being brainwashed or in a cult." Char laughed. "I'm sure you've heard it before too. But we make it work. Why? Because next to my sobriety, she's my top priority. God, I love that woman!" Char's face lit up with joy. "And she loves me in spite of all my, as we like to say, character defects. We make it work because we want it to work.

"I don't know about you and your man. Early days, right?"

Billy nodded. He didn't say *Even earlier than early days. If I'm lucky, we're like a just-fertilized egg in the womb.*

"Well, all I can say is that if this is going somewhere—and I think it is 'cause I saw the passion in your eyes and heard it in your words when you shared—you'll work things out so that you can both protect what's important, as well as be there for the other.

"Try to make him understand. But if you want my advice—and I know you didn't ask for it, but I love to give it—don't try to draw him into the program. Keep things a little separate. One thing is—normies and us just can't ever completely 'get' each other, not in my experience. That's why, even if this becomes soul mate territory for you, with a white picket fence and a shared Frenchie, you'll never be able to get from him what you get from the rooms. Because we're your people. Always. And these meetings, the steps, your sponsor, all that good shit will help keep you the best man you can be—for him."

"Wow. Thanks, Char. I think you've helped me more than you know."

"It weren't nothin'." She grinned.

They both knew it was something. But that was the beauty and the miracle of the program. They helped each other out with no more than a desire to be free and to share that freedom with another lost soul.

What Char had done this morning was momentous, but all in a day's work too.

Billy hugged her. "Let's do coffee sometime."

"Sure thing, Billy. Take care."

And she was gone. Billy watched her drive away in her little green-and-white electric Smart car and found the thing he'd found the very first time he'd stepped into a meeting: *hope*.

CHAPTER 19

THERE WAS something different the next time Milt saw Billy. It wasn't anything extraordinary. In fact, what made it special was its very ordinariness.

A couple of days after Dane had gone back home to Ohio and the acute pain and joy of his visit had quieted to something gentle yet throbbing, like an old scar, Billy simply showed up on his doorstep early one morning.

Milt had just taken Ruby out for a long walk, all the way around the perimeter of the park, which was about three miles all told. The weather forecast for that day predicted unseasonable heat for late winter, with late-afternoon temperatures soaring up to the low nineties, so Milt thought getting Ruby's major walk out of the way early was not only a good idea but a vital one. The walk was perfection—they started off just as the sun was coming up, with the sky on fire with color—pink, lavender, tangerine. A gilded band winked on the horizon. There was a gentle breeze, almost a whisper of air with just a hint of chill to it. There was quiet, blessed peaceful quiet.

Milt had a feeling, in this serenity, that circumstances in his life had done a one-eighty. Taking in the silhouetted palms and the mystical soaring mountain ranges gave him a sense of contentment he hadn't allowed himself to experience—until today.

At home, he was deciding what to do about breakfast when the kitchen door swung open. Billy poked his head in the doorway. "I know, I know. I should knock, but we're old buddies, right? Open-door policy among friends?"

Milt, at the sink, shook his head in mock dismay, pretending to be appalled at Billy's social graces. "Seriously? You just swing the door open? I could have been in here naked, jacking off or something." He chuckled.

"Well, isn't that a pretty picture!" Billy laughed. "If you're trying to discourage me from barging in, you're taking the wrong approach." He hesitated there in the open doorway. "Um, *can* I barge in?"

"You're already halfway there, you big doofus. Get in here."

And Billy did. Milt looked him over from head to toe. Internally, he gave a low whistle. Billy had something in common with the mountain ranges surrounding the valley, in that Milt never grew tired of the majesty of the view. He always appreciated it.

He suddenly realized he always appreciated Billy too, and the pleasure he found, if he let himself, in simply gazing at him. Today his tan skin and blond hair had a glow about them. The white shorts and sky-blue tank top emphasized his luminance, making his eyes look even bluer. It wasn't a new thought, but one Milt had had over and over. Billy was a beautiful man. The difference was that this morning, for the first time, Milt allowed himself the feeling.

He appreciated and admired without guilt, minus a nagging sense of betrayal.

He felt liberated.

Yet aside from how Milt felt, he sensed something different about Billy too. There was a quality Milt couldn't quite put his finger on. Perhaps it was a sense of ease, of joy, of being comfortable in his own skin that hadn't always been there. Or if it had, Milt hadn't witnessed it.

Whatever was going on, there was a new comfort with the two of them being together on an ordinary day in Milt's kitchen. Even Ruby seemed more at ease, not jumping on Billy for once but calmly regarding him from her bed in the corner of the living room. It was almost as though Billy belonged here. It was like Ruby felt Billy was *home*.

Milt washed his hands and then dried them on a dish towel. He turned to Billy. "You come scrounging around for breakfast?"

"Hey! That's not nice."

Milt chuckled. "Well, the timing is right."

"What did you have in mind?" Billy's gaze roamed the counter, the range. They were both empty.

"We could go out," Milt suggested. "Elmer's on Palm Canyon? I like their omelets."

Billy moved close. "I don't want to go out."

Milt edged closer. "I don't either. Not really." He smiled. "And anyway, I need to get to Trader Joe's." He turned to open his refrigerator. It was embarrassingly bare. "All out of eggs." He shrugged, slammed shut the refrigerator. "Scrambled eggs are about all I do for breakfast." He had a flash of an orange Fiesta plate with a stack of banana pecan pancakes on it. They were Corky's specialty and were always light, fluffy, and mouthwateringly delicious. In his mind's eye, he could see steam rising from the stack, a big pat of butter melting, sliding off to the side.

Milt forced the image out of his mind.

"I could, uh, pour you a bowl of cereal. I've got Lucky Charms." Milt allowed himself to stare at Billy with undisguised desire. Sexual tension thrummed in the air. Milt wanted to draw the conclusion that its arrival was sudden, but he knew, intuitively, that it had been there from the moment Billy boldly opened the door without knocking. And maybe, if he was being honest, much longer ago than that. Perhaps it had begun on that one disastrous yet magical day when Billy had cast himself as Milt's true-life hero....

Or perhaps it was simply because Milt was letting his true feelings out to play for the first time in a long, long time. He felt like years had been stripped away from his age—he could be a kid again, teens, early twenties.

He tried to reach down to discreetly adjust his dick, which had gotten hard.

Billy noticed. He pressed close to Milt, shoving his hand aside. He gave Milt's basket a squeeze. "Are these your Lucky Charms? If so, I'd consider myself very lucky indeed if I could get myself a serving." He squeezed again and let go. "A big serving." Billy's voice came out almost breathless, a croak.

Milt's jaw dropped. But he didn't move away.

Milt knew that once upon a time, maybe even as recently as a few days ago, his impulse would have been to back away from Billy with a mumble of apology.

To perhaps blush and laugh—and then go to the pantry and pull out the real Lucky Charms. And yes, there *was* a box there, right next to the box of Count Chocula. In some ways, Milt never did grow up.

But that was another day, another time. Another Milt.

Today simply felt different, washed new.

Milt thrust his hips outward and up a little, more fully into Billy's hand. Just that movement caused his heart to race, his knees to weaken, and his focus to blur just a little. There seemed no recourse for the moment other than to lean in and kiss Billy.

Their lips came together awkwardly, laughably. In his head Milt had a strange thought. *I want him to sing "My Funny Valentine" for me sometime.* It seemed, for just one moment, neither of them knew what to do. Open lips or closed? A peck or a lingering, full-throttle kiss?

The one thing Milt knew for certain—even though it had been a long time since he'd found himself in such a situation with a man—was don't ask, just do.

So he opened his mouth and went in for a kiss of the full-throttle variety. Billy's mouth, even this early in the morning, was clean, delightfully sweet, tasting faintly of mint. Their tongues dueled, and the dance was graceful. Billy's blond whiskers, not all that visible, were, however, tactile, feeling rough, sexy against Milt's face. Milt thought he could almost—almost—be satisfied with simply standing here and kissing him. Holding him close. There was a discreet kind of magic in simply holding him, feeling this solidity of another human being close.

It had been so long! He felt like a man who'd been dying of thirst suddenly getting water. The slaking of his need approached the province of miracle. Milt thought, for these past several months, that he'd never have this again. And yet here the gift of Billy had been, not so patiently waiting, all along. All Milt had to do was open his arms and accept.

He pulled away for a moment to stare into Billy's crystalline gaze. "You've been here the whole time, haven't you?" Milt felt a rush of emotion he couldn't quite label. Was he feeling joy? Hope? Desire?

In the end, labels didn't matter. The electric happiness coursing through him was enough. It didn't need a name, did it?

"What do you mean?" Billy asked.

"Never mind. I think I was asking that question more of myself." He took Billy's face in his hands. "Do you want to go in the bedroom?"

"Do you think we're moving too fast?" Billy wondered.

"Too fast? Too fast?" Milt laughed. "Are you kidding? I think we've maybe been moving too slow." He sighed. "I've been so caught up in grief, in mourning, in wondering if I could ever feel *anything* again, if I was even allowed to feel anything again, that I failed to see the wonderful thing that was right before my eyes. That wonderful thing is you, Billy Blue. It's you." Milt didn't know if he wanted to laugh or cry. Could he dare to do both?

He was free to do whatever he pleased! He was his own man.

Billy pulled away slightly, letting Milt's caressing hands drop away. He looked up at Milt shyly. His voice was soft, gentle when he spoke. "No. We haven't been moving too slow. Although I'd be lying if I said I hadn't thought that same thing many, many times. But Milt, honey, you needed that time to process your pain."

Billy shook his head. "And you may never get over that pain, not completely. I accept that. And you have to as well. I think you're beginning to—and that fills my heart with joy. But no to the too slow. Just right. Just absolutely right. Things come to us when we're ready."

Milt smiled. "How did you get to be so wise?"

"Ah. I don't know about that." Billy looked a little abashed—the reddish glow at his cheeks making him look even more handsome. He cocked his head. "Is that trip to the bedroom still on offer?"

Milt smiled and wrapped his arms around Billy, pulling him close once more so that their bodies were almost one—in alignment. Milt nodded and then pressed his forehead to Billy's. "What about breakfast?"

"Hmmm. I think I need to work up a little more appetite first." And Billy broke away, took Milt's hand, and led him back to the bedroom.

CHAPTER 20

IT HAD only been a couple of weeks, yet Billy felt like he'd been with Milt for a long, long time. When he stood next to him, there was something solid there, a sense that Milt wasn't going anywhere.

And neither was Billy.

Since that morning two weeks and two days ago, when Billy had emboldened himself to simply enter Milt's trailer without knocking, they'd seldom been apart. Billy's own trailer had an air of neglect—the only movement dust motes floating in shafts of sunlight. The bed, unmade, stayed unmade. The dishes, stacked neatly in the drainer on the counter next to the sink, remained there. The jute window shade above Billy's bed remained at half-mast—forever.

Other than to pick up clothes and toiletries, Billy hadn't been back. It simply no longer felt like home, because Milt and Ruby weren't there. Home wasn't a place, Billy reasoned, but where the things and people you loved were. He suddenly felt, maybe for the first time, that he had a place to be. And that was a very good thing.

They'd come together that morning a couple of weeks ago like two practiced souls. Or an old married couple. A couple that continued to take pleasure in each other's bodies, knowing, comfortably, exactly which buttons to push (and lick and caress) to bring the other absolute joy. They'd simply merged. It was as though they'd already mapped and memorized the contours of each other's bodies. Where with past lovers there had been gracelessness and awkwardness at first, taking time to get into the groove of wants and needs, Billy didn't find that to be true with Milt. Their intimate choreography was flawless—maybe because the emotion backing it up allowed for no error. How could there be mistakes when you cared so much? When there existed so much passion?

They'd made love every night and every morning since Billy had moved in. Only once had this unspoken decision to be so totally together been brought up. Billy recalled the short conversation now, standing in biting cold and fluttering snowflakes on top of a hill, surrounded by tombstones.

"Do you think we're being rash?" Milt had asked one sun-drenched morning, wrapped in sheets slightly damp with sweat.

It was maybe the third day of what Billy thought of as their union. Their bodies were close, slick with sweat and come. Billy's head was on Milt's chest. Milt's arm was wrapped around him. Billy was just beginning to drift off into blessed early morning sleep with the thought *There's no place I'd rather be. In all the wonderful places of the world I could choose, this is where*

I'd pick. The best. "Rash? You don't have a rash, do you? You didn't get it from me!" Billy laughed, snuggling closer, smelling the clean scent on Milt's neck.

"C'mon. I'm serious. I know what Dane would say."

"What would Dane say?" Billy had a feeling, just from Milt making this statement, that Dane would say something very sensible. He wasn't wrong in his guess.

"Dane would say that we should slow down. He'd say 'act in haste, repent at leisure.' He'd say that we should take our time and get to know each other before jumping into living together."

"Living together? Is that what we're doing?" Billy asked, mock wonder in his tone.

Milt tweaked his nipple. "You know we are. It's only a matter of time before you give up that Airstream over there."

"You think so, huh? Think you're my forever guy? Because I got to tell you, Milt, I wouldn't live with someone unless I believed he was my forever guy."

Milt had been quiet for a long while in reaction, Billy thought, to his words about forever. Finally Milt sighed. "Yeah. I know this is something, what we have here. I know it not in my head so much, but in my heart. My head tells me all the things Dane would say. But my heart knows. The heart always knows what it wants, what it needs." Milt turned a little to look into Billy's eyes. "*Who* it needs. What matters."

Those words had started their second, slow round of lovemaking. And when Billy had awakened from a long second sleep, he knew he was there to stay. The logistics only needed to be worked out.

Would he have taken this trip with Milt if he hadn't been sure they were solid?

Yesterday morning they'd flown from Palm Springs to Pittsburgh, ostensibly so Milt could show Billy from where he came, but really to have the meeting they were having right now, this impossibly cold and snowy afternoon in early March.

They stood in front of a dark granite tombstone, polished, simple, rectangular. On it were the words Cornelius "Corky" Abbott, 1959-2017. Next to Corky's name and dates were Milt's: Milton Grabaur 1976- and a blank space.

Dark, bruised slate-gray clouds hung low on the horizon, promising more snow than the flakes already dancing in the wind. The tree-covered hills, naked, reached up to a dappled sky, hungry for the patches of sun that would occasionally appear, taunting.

"Does it bother you that I'll be buried here? Next to Corky?"

Billy looked over at Milt, who hadn't moved his gaze from the tombstone as he posed his question. Billy witnessed the tears standing in Milt's eyes, waiting to fall. Or maybe they were frozen in place—it was cold enough.

And Billy wondered if it *did* bother him. He processed awhile before answering. "Honestly, a part of me thinks that it should. But it doesn't. Corky was part of your history. Corky made you the kind, gentle, and caring man I've come to love. So I thank him. And the least I can do is let you lie next to him when your time comes. No, Milt, I'm not jealous. You loved him."

"I love you." Milt quickly glanced over at Billy.

"I know. And your being laid to rest here someday doesn't change that, not one bit." Deep in his heart, Billy never believed in things like final resting places and tombstones anyway. Those things were for the shells of stuff left behind. If there was an afterlife, there were no physical bodies, only the energy, light, and love that animated us.

Milt nodded but seemed uncertain.

A harsh wind, icy, blew out of the north, making them shiver. Billy had grown so used to the weather of the desert and Southern California that he'd forgotten how biting and bone-chilling temperatures like this could be. The cold actually hurt. He'd quickly revised his notion of hell from blistering, fiery heat to cold like this for eternity. He rubbed his arms up and down, trying to stimulate warmth, circulation. "Can we go? I'm freezing. You said there was a diner downtown that served french fries with gravy. That sounds awesome." Billy was trying not to plead.

"Sure. Can you just give me a moment here alone? You can go back to the rental, crank up the heat, check your Facebook." Milt smiled.

"You sure?"

"Yeah. I'd like a moment here." Milt's gaze went back to the tombstone, yet it was faraway, as though he was seeing something that wasn't there.

"Okay." Billy bit his tongue to prevent himself from exhorting Milt not to take too long. Not because he was jealous, but because it was so cold. Frostbite and hypothermia were real things. And neither of them had appropriate outerwear for this. Billy wore only a hoodie, over which he'd added a denim jacket. He had no gloves, hat, or scarf.

He trudged back up the hill, passing tombstones and markers and looking down over one shoulder at the little town of Summitville below him. Chimneys belched smoke. Traffic moved slowly on the main arteries, taking care. The Ohio River curved just beyond

the edge of the town, brown/green and glinting now
and then when the sun deigned to put in an appearance.
On its banks bare-limbed trees reached up to the sky,
their branches skeletal fingers.

He got in the rental, a black Hyundai Sonata, started it up, and cranked the heat to high, even though all
that accomplished at the moment was for the fan to
blow even more cold air on him.

Ah well, Billy had learned to be both patient and
to live in hope.

As the car gradually, too slowly in Billy's humble
opinion, heated up, he turned to watch Milt at the grave.
His broad shoulders tested the seams of the long black
coat he wore. Even though his back was to Billy, Billy
could detect the movement of his jaw. *He's talking to
Corky. I wonder what he's saying. Is he talking about
me?* Billy laughed to himself at the absurdity and self-
ishness of his thoughts.

Billy knew that whatever Milt was saying was
none of his business. Milt had a history. So did Billy. And what lay in those former days and years made
them the men they were now. Billy wouldn't have had
it any other way.

He brought his iPhone to life, checked to see if
he had internet, and opened his browser. The closest
AA meeting was late afternoon, near Pittsburgh. Billy
would have to get himself there. It had been a long time
since he'd been to a meeting anywhere other than Palm
Springs, so it might be a little weird, but probably not.
Wherever you went, Billy thought, there you were. And
meetings were the same everywhere, although peopled
by different characters. Essentially they were about
folks who'd discovered a miracle generously sharing

it with others with the same affliction. Nah, it wouldn't be weird at all.

He had not let sobriety lose its priority. He wouldn't. He couldn't. He wanted to be his best self not only for Milt but also for himself.

He set the phone in his lap, reclined the seat, and closed his eyes as heat, blessed heat, washed over him.

CHAPTER 21

CORKY SAT on the tombstone in front of Milt, his legs stretched out in front of him. Although dressed in a pair of gray wool slacks, a pressed button-down white cotton shirt, and a black-and-white checkered sweater vest, he didn't appear cold. No, he looked relaxed, arms folded across his chest. His bare head was covered with a black fedora, rakishly angled. Corky always was a bit of a dandy when it came to clothes. His dark eyes twinkled, even though the sun, when it deigned to come out, was behind him.

Milt knew, of course, that Corky wasn't really there, sitting atop his own tombstone at the Hilltop Cemetery in Summitville, Ohio.

And yet he was, because Milt was certain of one thing—Corky still existed; a piece of his loving energy would always be intertwined in Milt's heart and soul. So Corky couldn't really be dead. No, not ever.

Mystical musings aside, Milt had come all this way, spending far more than he could afford, because he had a few things to say to Corky. Milt felt the only way to convey them was in person.

He'd begun casually. "How are things? You know, in the afterlife. Is it what you expected?"

"Pancakes every night for supper," Corky said and winked. "It never gets cold. And the beds here? They're *real* heavenly beds, honey." Corky shrugged. "It's as okay as it can be, without you."

Milt nodded. "Do you watch me?"

"Like on TV? Or what was that movie we saw once? With that Jim Carrey?"

"*The Truman Show*."

Corky nodded. "That's it." His gaze took on a far-away cast. "Maybe at first, I was involved with you. I needed to see what you were doing. But honestly, my sweetheart, the time I spent on you became less and less as I realized your earthly concerns weren't mine. Not anymore. It's not that you stop caring, man, it's that you realize the important stuff—the love—never goes away, no matter the minutia going on down there or up there or wherever." Corky laughed. "I'm not in a place, you know."

"I think I do. It's good to see you clear-headed, smart, like you used to be."

"Thank you. Thank you for taking care of me when that 'smart' man you refer to was buried inside. I was always there, my sweet man. I knew everything you did. The hell of it was I could never let you know I knew."

Milt's breath caught. He squeezed his eyes shut to ebb the flow of sudden tears.

"Don't cry."

Milt shook his head. "I knew. I knew." He laughed. "That's why I put up with all of your shit. And we are *not* talking metaphorically here."

They both had a good laugh over that. They were perhaps the only two people who could.

"But seriously, I had this sense, deep inside, that you were always there, even when you seemed most lost."

"You were right."

They said nothing for a while. The wind picked up, and it seemed that Corky's image wavered a little with it, the edges fragmenting and then coming back together.

When the wind died down, Corky said, "I know."

"You know what?" Milt asked, heat rising to his cheeks despite the arctic chill in the air. He knew.

"Let's not play games. I left all that behind."

"He's a nice guy."

"I know that too." Corky smiled, and suddenly he felt much closer, although he stayed where he was. "You love him."

"I think I do."

"No, you do."

"Is that okay?"

"Don't be stupid, Milt." And Milt felt a little slap to the back of his head. He rubbed it, smiling at Corky. "What do you think? There's only so much love in the world? That you have to be careful how you portion it so you don't run out?"

Milt wanted to say something, but the words stuck in his throat.

"Love is what the whole world is made of. It's all there is. And there's no end to it. You'll get to this on your own, very soon, but I'll just tell you now—your love for him doesn't diminish in the least your love for me. You have enough. You *always* have enough."

Milt nodded, closing his eyes for just a moment to savor an image of Billy in his head. It was that first time he saw him, when he came to help him out when his trailer flooded. There was someone who cared. He knew too that savoring this image wasn't wrong. Corky could see it, Milt believed, in his head and approved. Because it made Milt happy.

When he opened his eyes, all he saw was the black grave marker, the dried and yellow grass hidden here and there under patches of dirty snow and ice, and a sky that had turned threatening, with blackish clouds gathering.

The snow began coming down harder.

Milt took one more look at the tombstone and hurried to the car, where he smiled at the vision of Billy asleep in the passenger seat.

As he was reaching for the door handle, he swore he felt, very soft, a gentle kiss planted on the top of his head.

He paused to look up at the sky, and swear to God, the clouds parted for just one moment to reveal a spear of golden sunlight.

And a butterfly, its wings yellow and cobalt blue, fluttered past his vision to disappear into the snow.

He opened the door, and Billy roused, looking over at Milt and smiling. "Okay?"

"Okay. Let's go."

Milt started the car and drove off, confidently, into the blizzard.

KEEP READING FOR AN EXCERPT FROM

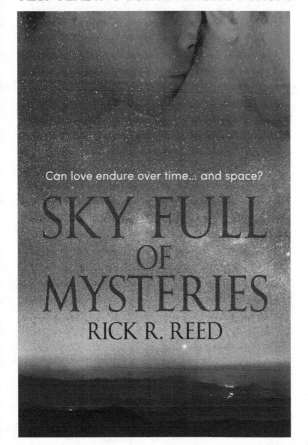

Can love endure over time... and space?

SKY FULL
OF
MYSTERIES
RICK R. REED

SKY FULL OF MYSTERIES

By Rick R. Reed

What if your first love was abducted and presumed dead—but returned twenty years later?

That's the dilemma Cole Weston faces. Now happily married to Tommy D'Amico, he's suddenly thrown into a surreal world when his first love, Rory Schneidmiller, unexpectedly reappears.

Where has Rory been all this time? Has he time-traveled? What happened to him two decades ago, when a strange mass appeared in the night sky and lifted him into outer space? Rory has no memory of those years. For him, it's as though only a day or two has passed.

Rory still loves Cole with the passion unique to young first love. Cole has never forgotten Rory, yet Tommy has been his rock, by his side since Rory disappeared.

Cole is forced to choose between an idealized and passionate first love and the comfort of a long-term marriage. How can he decide? Who faces this kind of quandary, anyway? The answers might lie among the stars....

www.dreamspinnerpress.com

CHAPTER 1

AFTER THEY made love, they were polar opposites in how they reacted.

Cole, barely minutes after coming, would be asleep, mouth open and snoring, body lax. A baby who'd just been fed. Rory looked down on him as he sat perched with his back against the headboard. Despite—or maybe because of—the spittle that ran out of one side of Cole's mouth, he felt a shock of warmth go through him as he gazed at Cole, wondering how he'd gotten so lucky. Although Rory was a few years younger, he was a nerd with glasses. He wasn't bad-looking; he just wasn't all that noticeable in a crowd. How had he snared a guy like Cole, with his perfect runner's build, his dark brown wavy hair, and the perpetual five-o'clock shadow that accentuated, rather than hid, the angular planes of his face and his sharp jawline. Rory snickered in the darkness at Cole as a snore erupted from him, almost loud enough to shake the glass in their bedroom window.

It was always like this—maniac in the sack until he came, and then it was lights out for Cole, as though he'd been drugged.

Rory, on the other hand, always felt energized, pumped up, alive, as if he should hop from the bed, go outside, and run a mile or three. Or make a meal. Or write the great American novel. Or catalog his collection of books alphabetically, and then by genre.

Tonight was no different. They'd just moved into the one-bedroom apartment in Chicago's Rogers Park neighborhood. The neighborhood, the Windy City's farthest east and north before heading into suburbia, afforded them a chance to live by Lake Michigan without the higher rents they'd encounter closer to downtown.

They were young and in love, and cohabitating was a first for both of them. Rory felt they were already having their happy-ever-after moment.

The apartment was a find—a vintage courtyard building east of Sheridan Road on Fargo Avenue. Their unit's bedroom faced Lake Michigan, which was only a few steps away from their front door. A lake view, high ceilings, crown molding, formal dining room with a built-in hutch, huge living room with working fireplace, and an original bathroom with an enormous claw-foot tub were just a few of the amenities they were delighted to find—all for the "steal" monthly rent of only five hundred dollars.

The apartment, which would eventually be filled to bursting with a hodgepodge of furniture and belongings, ranging from family antiques supplied by Cole to *Lost in Space* action figures from Rory, was now a scene of chaos with moving boxes everywhere, almost none of them unpacked.

They'd spent the whole day moving and were exhausted when they were finished. Even though it was August, by the time they were done dragging the boxes out of their U-Haul truck, through their building's courtyard, and then up to the tenth floor via the rickety but thank-heaven-reliable elevator, the skies above the lake had gone dark. They ordered stuffed spinach pizza from Giordano's, just south of them on Sheridan, and feasted on it, melted mozzarella on their chins, on a couple of beach towels they found at the top of one of the boxes.

And of course, Rory being twenty-three and Cole twenty-six, with their blossoming love all of six months old, they did find the time and the energy to make love, once on the beach towels and once in their bed. Rory knew there'd be more of the same come morning's first light.

Ah, sweet youth.

But getting back to postcoital bliss, Rory now found himself feeling restless as he lay beside the snoring Cole. The moon was nearly full and they'd yet to put up blinds, so it shone in the bedroom window, casting the room in a kind of silvery opalescence. Rory thought the boxes and the furniture—Cole's oak sleigh bed and Rory's pair of maple tallboy dressers, plus an overstuffed chair they'd found in an alley just before moving—all had a kind of grayish aspect to them, almost unreal, as if he were observing his own bedroom as a scene from a black-and-white movie. Maybe something noir… with Barbara Stanwyck and Fred Mac-Murray. Rory smiled and turned away from Cole. Just a half hour or so earlier, with the overhead light fixture shining down on them, Rory thought the movie would have been a porno, with himself cast as the insatiable bottom.

He chuckled to himself.

He tried to relax, doing an old exercise he'd learned from his mom. Starting with his feet, he'd wiggle, tense, and then allow that body part to go slack to relax. He worked his way up his whole body, wiggling, tensing, and relaxing as he went, until he reached his head.

And—sigh—he was still wide-awake.

Behind him, though, as if he had eyes in the back of his head, he noticed something odd.

It was like there was suddenly a waxing and waning of light.

Rory turned and looked toward the uncovered window. He couldn't quite see the moon, but it seemed like it was brightening and darkening, brightening, then darkening….

But the whole of this August day, it had been clear, with nary a cloud in the sky. Rory wondered if a cloud bank had moved in, obscuring the moon and then revealing it as the wind pushed it away. He could see this in his mind's eye but couldn't quite believe it.

The light was simply too brilliant. At its brightest, the whole room lit up, as though he'd switched on the overhead fixture. Rory was surprised Cole didn't awaken. Or maybe he wasn't so surprised after all. Rory had spent enough nights with his "great dark man" to know his slumber habits. When Cole drifted off, which he did effortlessly and with amazing speed, there was little that would wake him. Rory thought they could have a New Orleans jazz band march through their bedroom and all Cole would do, at most, was maybe turn over… or snort a little.

He lightly kissed Cole's cheek, undeterred by the scratch of Cole's scruff, and slid from the bed to peer out the window.

The lake was a great black expanse. The sky was only a few shades lighter than the water below it, with a slight yellowish tinge due to all the city lights. And the moon, just shy of full, shimmered, a lovely yellow-gold, completely unobscured by clouds. If Rory squinted just right, he thought he could just about make out a face in the surface of that moon....

The sky simply had no clouds to offer that night.

Rory stepped back from the window and glanced back at his slumbering man. *So why was the light getting brighter and then darker?* He turned to the window and peered outside again. If not for the city's light pollution, he was certain he'd see entire constellations of stars. He allowed his eyes to adjust a bit and saw more detail below, along Fargo beach. The water was not exactly black, after all. The waves, small and unimpressive due to the lack of wind, still managed to toss up a few whitecaps, especially near the shore, which looked grayer in the darkness. The beach, and the island of boulders just a few laps beyond it, took on more definition, enough that it made Rory come to a decision.

If he couldn't sleep, he might as well take the opportunity to go outside, enjoy the warm breezes and what appeared to be a deserted beachfront.

He dressed quickly and silently—even though he knew he needn't have bothered since Cole was beyond waking—in a pair of cutoffs and a Doctor Who T-shirt. He slid his feet into flip-flops, grabbed his keys off the dresser, and headed for the front door.

Other than the steady *whoosh* of traffic on Sheridan Road to the west, the night was quiet. Rory wished he'd checked the time before heading out, but judging from the silence all around him, he'd guess it was the wee small hours of the morning, maybe 2:00 or 3:00 a.m. This was Chicago, after all. There was usually someone stumbling around, even in blackest night.

But his street was empty. The tree branches and their leaves cast shadows on the silvery pavement beneath his feet because of the moon's brightness. His footsteps, even in flip-flops, sounded extra loud as he headed east, toward the beach.

At the end of the street, there was a cul-de-sac where cars could turn around, and beyond that, a set of stone steps that led down to the sand. Rory stood at the top of the steps, looking out at the sand and water, the pile of boulders just offshore that Cole promised he'd swim out to the next day with Rory. A white lifeguard chair, empty, sat crookedly in the sand, leaning as it sunk to the left. The moon shone brilliantly on the water, laying a swath of golden light upon its gently undulating surface. If Rory looked at this light just right, perhaps squinting a bit behind his glasses, he could almost imagine the light rising up, like an illuminated fountain, from the water's surface.

He took the steps quickly and was on the sand in seconds. He kicked off his flip-flops and sighed when he felt the cool sand squishing up between his toes. He looked around once more, paying particular attention to the concrete that bordered the beach, to assure himself he had the gift of a city beach all to himself.

And he did. He did!

He tore off his shirt, set it down, and then removed his glasses, placing them on top of the T-shirt. With a little cry, he dashed toward the water, a small laugh escaping his lips. He stopped briefly at its edge, gasping at the icy cold of the waves, even this late in the summer, as they ran up to meet him, lapping and biting at his toes. And then he took a deep breath, waded in up to his knees, and paused to consider if he really wanted to go whole hog.

What the hell.

He waded in a little farther, until the bottom dropped out from under him suddenly and instead of the water reaching to the top of his thighs, hit him just above his belly button. It was freezing! And Rory knew there was only one solution: get full immersion over as quickly as possible.

He raised his hands over his head and dove as a wave rolled in toward him. The world went silent as he went under, the murky depths of the water almost black. He held his breath as long as he could, swimming outward. His mother's voice erupted in his head, scolding, telling him to go back to shore because it was late and there was no one around. What if he, God forbid, got a cramp?

Rory shushed his mother and continued to swim toward Michigan or whatever was directly opposite, hundreds of miles away. He swam until he felt his lungs would burst.

And then he surfaced, shaking the water from his hair. The first thing he noticed was how full immersion had done the trick—he wasn't exactly warm, but the water temperature was at least bearable.

The second was the light on the water. It had changed to a strange pale radiance, a shifting, silvery opalescence that, in addition to his recent underwater swimming, left him nearly breathless.

He trod water and hazarded a glimpse up at the sky, expecting to see the moon and perhaps that bank of clouds that had managed to elude him earlier.

But the moon was gone. Or at least hidden.

Is this real?

Rory couldn't believe what he was seeing. He actually slipped under for a helpless moment because both his arms and feet stopped moving. He came back up quickly, sputtering and spitting out lake water, gaze fixed on the sky.

"What the fuck?" he whispered.

Was what he saw natural? Like, as in a natural phenomenon? What was above him appeared like some membrane, formed from smoky gray clouds, but alive. It rose up, mountainous, into the night sky. As he peered closer at the form, it seemed to almost breathe, to expand in and out. And within the gray smoke or fog, figures seemed to be spinning. They were black and amorphous, like shadows brought to life. The fact that the cloud—or whatever it was—cast an otherworldly silvery light from below didn't make the figures any more distinctive.

This can't be real. I'm back at the apartment right now, sound asleep next to Cole. That pizza really did a number on me. Rory knew his notions were simply wishful thinking.

The membrane or cloud or whatever one wanted to call it was as real as the moon had been above him.

The black figures, spinning, began, one by one, to drop. They were too far distant for Rory to hear any splashes, but he could plainly see that some of them were disconnecting from the membrane or cloud or whatever one wanted to call it and plopping down into the placid surface of Lake Michigan.

Because of its immensity, Rory was unable to determine if the thing above him was close by or distant. It could have been hovering directly overhead. Or it might have been as far away as downtown or even the western edge of Indiana. Perhaps it was some industrial disaster thrown up by the city of Gary? Perhaps it was a military experiment, a new kind of aircraft?

And of course Rory, ever the science fiction geek, came to the last supposition almost reluctantly, because it terrified him—perhaps it was some sort of alien vessel, a UFO in everyday parlance. The kind of thing Rory had both dreaded and hoped to bear witness to almost all of his young life.

He stared at it in wonder, lost for a moment in time. He hoped he'd gain more clarity on what the thing was, but the longer he stared, the more confusing it became. Was it some freak of nature? Some hitherto unseen cloud formation? Was it really a spaceship beyond his or anyone's wildest imagination?

Whatever it was, he was certain it was warming the water around him, which led him to the conclusion that it must have some powerful energy to heat up a body of water as large as Lake Michigan. What had been cold, now felt almost as warm as bathwater.

And that scared Rory just as much as this monstrously huge thing in the sky above him. What if the water continued to heat up? What if it reached the boiling point and he was poached alive in it?

What if the black, shadowy beings he witnessed spinning within the mist meant him harm as they dropped from the cloud? What if they were, right now, swimming toward him, all bulbous heads and soulless gray eyes?

He shuddered in spite of the warmth of the water around him. He leveled himself out, lowered his face to the water, and began the fastest crawl he could manage toward shore, which suddenly seemed impossibly far away.

And a new fear seized him as he paddled, panting, through the dark water—what if something as prosaic as drowning claimed him? Would they ever find him?

What would Cole do when he woke at last, to find himself in bed and alone? What would he do as the sun rose, lighting up their little love nest, and there was no Rory?

Rory didn't want to see the thing anymore. Just looking at it induced in him a feeling of dread so powerful, it nauseated him. So he kept his face in the water, only turning his head to the side every few strokes to grab a breath of air, until he neared the shore. He squatted low, panting hard, in the shallows and at last hazarded a glance up at the sky.

It was empty.

Save for a muted orange glow from light pollution and the moon, now distant, there was nothing in the sky. Rory crawled from the water and plopped down on the damp sand at the lake's edge.

Had it simply been a hallucination? Or maybe there *had* been a cloud bank, a thunderhead maybe, and his sci-fi geek's mind had transformed it into something much more wondrous? And much more threatening?

He shivered and rubbed his hands up and down his bare arms to warm himself. After a while, when he felt he was ready, he stood on shaky legs, the comparison to a newly born colt not lost on him, and staggered over to where he'd left his T-shirt and glasses. He yanked the tee over his head and put the glasses—chunky horn-rims—onto his face. He'd been wearing glasses since he was five years old. It felt more natural with them on than without.

It crossed his mind for half a second that his blurry vision had been a contributor to what he'd seen—or not seen; he was already doubting himself—but even with the glasses restoring his vision to twenty-twenty, the view of the sky above remained placid, dark, unremarkable.

He scanned the horizon for a while, still looking for something he'd lost, but saw nothing new other than an industrial ship way out there, at the very edge of what Rory imagined was the world.

Perhaps the ship would topple off the edge and into the mouth of a waiting giant membrane that looked something like a cloud with lights and spinning figures inside?

Rory thought he should laugh at the notion but couldn't quite bring himself to. He walked slowly across the sand. It wasn't until he got halfway up the steps to the street that he realized he'd left his flip-flops on the beach.

He hurried back to claim them. As he was stooping over to grab them, he noticed a dog running toward him. It was a black Labrador, or something like it, because it appeared as if it was some kind of charging shadow.

It rushed by him without slowing to sniff or in any way regard him. "Hey!" Rory called after the animal, which ignored him. Rory looked around to see if there was a frazzled owner, leash in hand, running after the dog, but the beach was empty.

When he looked back, the dog was gone.

Could it have been one of the dark figures that dropped from the cloud?

Rory froze at the middle of the stairs. The thought chilled him. The whole idea of his sanity suddenly came into question.

He hurried up the rest of the stairs and headed back toward his apartment. He hoped Cole hadn't awakened and gone looking for him.

As he neared the courtyard of the building, he decided, unless he couldn't avoid it, he would keep this whole weird episode to himself.

As he headed for his front door, he thought things would look better, more rational, in the light of day.

Right?

Teacher Dane Bernard is a gentle giant, loved by all at Summitville High School. He has a beautiful wife, two kids, and an easy rapport with staff and students alike. But Dane has a secret, one he expects to keep hidden for the rest of his life—he's gay.

But when he loses his wife, Dane finally confronts his attraction to men. And a new teacher, Seth Wolcott, immediately catches his eye. Seth himself is starting over, licking his wounds from a breakup. The last thing Seth wants is another relationship—but when he spies Dane on his first day at Summitville High, his attraction is immediate and electric.

As the two men enter into a dance of discovery and new love, they're called upon to come to the aid of bullied gay student Truman Reid. Truman is out and proud, which not everyone at his small-town high school approves of. As the two men work to help Truman ignore the bullies and love himself without reservation, they all learn life-changing lessons about coming out, coming to terms, acceptance, heartbreak, and falling in love.

www. dreamspinnerpress.com

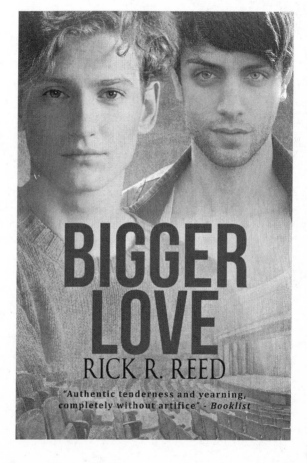

BIGGER
LOVE

RICK R. REED

"Authentic tenderness and yearning,
completely without artifice" - *Booklist*

Sequel to *Big Love*

Truman Reid is Summitville High's most out-and-proud senior. He can't wait to take his fierce, uncompromising self away from his small Ohio River hometown, where he's suffered more than his share of bullying. He's looking forward to bright lights and a big city. Maybe he'll be the first gender-fluid star to ever win an Academy Award. But all that changes on the first day of school when he locks eyes with the most gorgeous hunk he's ever seen.

Mike Stewart, big, dark-haired, and with the most amazing blue eyes, is new to town. He's quiet, manly, and has the sexy air of a lost soul. It's almost love at first sight for Truman. He thinks that love could deepen when Mike becomes part of the stage crew for *Harvey*, the senior class play Truman's directing. But is Mike even gay? And how will it work when Truman's mother is falling for Mike's dad?

Plus Truman, never the norm, makes a daring and controversial choice for the production that has the whole town up in arms.

See how it all plays out on a stage of love, laughter, tears, and sticking up for one's essential self....

www. dreamspinnerpress.com